The Best Short Stories of
William Kittredge

Other Books by William Kittredge

Owning It All

Hole in the Sky: A Memoir

Who Owns the West?

The Nature of Generosity

Taking Care: Thoughts on Storytelling and Belief

The Portable Western Reader
  Editor

The Last Best Place: A Montana Anthology
  Editor with Annick Smith

the best short stories of

WILLIAM KITTREDGE

Graywolf Press
Saint Paul, Minnesota

Publication of this volume is made possible in part by a grant provided by the Minnesota State Arts Board, through an appropriation by the Minnesota State Legislature; a grant from the Wells Fargo Foundation Minnesota; and a grant from the National Endowment for the Arts. Significant support has also been provided by the Bush Foundation; Marshall Field's Project Imagine with support from the Target Foundation; the McKnight Foundation; and other generous contributions from foundations, corporations, and individuals. To these organizations and individuals we offer our heartfelt thanks.

NATIONAL
ENDOWMENT
FOR THE ARTS

MINNESOTA
STATE ARTS BOARD

Published by Graywolf Press
2402 University Avenue, Suite 203
Saint Paul, Minnesota 55114
All rights reserved.

www.graywolfpress.org
Published in the United States of America
Printed in Canada

ISBN 1-55597-384-1

2 4 6 8 9 7 5 3 1
First Graywolf Printing, 2003

Library of Congress Control Number: 2002111861

Cover design: Veto Design

Cover photograph: Getty Images

CONTENTS

The Best Short Stories of
William Kittredge

In this old beginning of the end, Streeter thinks about starting out in agriculture, and remembers coming home drunk from Winnemucca in the morning hours before daylight and finding a man named Andre Leeman sitting on the front steps and smoking a cigarette, his long chin and concave cheeks briefly illuminated when he touched the cigarette to his lips.

It was June and the barley crop was in the ground, and the alfalfa haying wouldn't start for another couple of weeks, a time of brief freedom that had led Streeter to a spate of drinking and running the back roads. This night had brought him miles from the tavern in Paradise Valley without much memory of more than sagebrush desert flowing at the edges of his headlights, and he was surprised by the year-old Ford pickup with a caved-in tailgate that was parked by his front gate, and then by the glow of cigarette over there on the concrete steps to the house.

"Takes you long enough," the man said, and then he told Streeter about being a flyer and wanting the brush-spraying contract. "Been sitting here six hours," he said, "which must mean something."

"Means you got more time than sense," Streeter said, almost at once hating the sourness of drink in himself, which led to such talk. So he offered this Andre Leeman a hit from the pint of Old Crow he was packing, and asked him to wait until the next day for any serious talk, and stumbled into the house and into his bedroom where his wife was sleeping with the two children in the bed, one on each side of her, and no room left for him.

Streeter went back to the living room and slept about an hour and a half on the couch, then slipped out so his wife wouldn't hear him and drove slowly to a circle of willows near the upper limits of his property, where the headgates were flowing with water out of the creek. The flyer, Andre Leeman, found him there just after noon, asleep and sweating in the sun with his feet hanging out the window on the driver's side of the pickup. He shook Streeter's foot.

"Been hunting all over for you," he said, when Streeter had got himself awake and washed his face in the cold water come off the snow in the Warner Mountains.

"Sorry," Streeter said, but this Andre Leeman had already gone limping off to his pickup. He came back with his own half-empty pint of Old Crow, and they sat together on the wooden frame of the headgate, resting in the sun and sipping whiskey and talking about the deal on the brush spraying.

Like most of those old-time spray pilots, Leeman flew an ancient Steerman biplane, one of those rough-looking remnants of the '20s and '30s with a massive stub-nosed radial engine and a maze of struts and wires between the wings, heavy-looking aircraft with an open cockpit where the pilots with their leather helmets and goggles looked like World War I flying aces, dropping their aircraft close to the earth in the stillness of an early morning and churning along over the cool dewy croplands, leaving an undulating path of misty chemical spray while their wheels sometimes skimmed the leaves. Leeman claimed to have inherited his Steerman from his father, who caught a Baptist church steeple while spraying cotton in Arkansas. The old man had been crippled for life, and the Steerman mostly wrecked, but now it was rebuilt and ready for work. Leeman didn't say why he had brought it so far from Arkansas to Idaho.

"I been around this all my life," he said. "I can do you good work, close down as anybody. I was in Korea, flying a little Piper, and they kicked me out." He shook his head over this bit of old history, as if the motives of some men and organizations were impossible to imagine. "I been doing this ever since," he said.

They finished the whiskey, and Streeter gave him the job. Leeman was new in the country and had nobody to vouch for him, but Streeter liked that hour or so in the sun, talking about foreign lands beyond the Pacific between little sips of whiskey, and that was reason enough.

A week later Leeman showed up with the old silver-painted Steerman and two boys to flag for him in the brush, one of them driving his Ford pickup with the crushed tailgate and the other bringing his '59 flatbed International truck with a 500-gallon mix tank chained down on the back. It was all shipshape, 3 yellow 55-gallon drums of chemical in the back of the pickup and the chain binder tied secure with heavy telephone-company wire.

It was early daybreak when Leeman buzzed the main house twice, and Streeter came floundering out of sleep and got himself down to the highway, wearing only house slippers on his feet, and no socks. Leeman brought the Steerman soft onto the narrow pitted asphalt, and taxied up to where Streeter stood and revved the radial engine to a crackling roar, and shut it down and grinned. Dust from the prop-wash settled out into the pretty morning, and the birds took up again and the day was perfect, with smoke rising in an unwavering string from the crooked pipe over one of the tin-sided houses where two of Streeter's ranch-hand pensioners batched together.

Leeman stood down off the wing of the Steerman, stretched like his back was aching, and rubbed his hands over his whisker stubble, then twanged one of the strut wires like he was tinkering with a stringed instrument. "She never lets me down," he said. "Not hard, anyways." He grinned at Streeter.

And things went fine. Leeman was good at his work. Streeter sent a man with him, to help out on the mix truck, pumping chemicals from the yellow concentrate drums to dilute with creek water in the big tank, and then over to the spray tanks on the Steerman. The contract was for spraying almost 4,000 acres of brush, on land where the native grasses had been killed out by overgrazing. Given time, with the sage knocked down, the feed would come back. That was the theory. The work involved endless trips with the Steerman and had to be done in the absolute stillness of early morning, so the spray would not drift.

By the time a gusty little breeze came up just before noon of that first day Leeman had already covered a little more than 300 acres, and he was staying down close, as a spray pilot should, and it was fine to watch in the clear light, the mist swirling out behind in the draft from the propeller and turning through bright rainbows over the smoky green of the sage. With any sort of luck the job wouldn't take more than ten days, or two weeks at the most.

Streeter asked Leeman to dinner that night, and Leeman showed up carrying another pint of whiskey, cleaned up and new shaven, with his hair slicked down. "Gift," Leeman said, and he shoved the flat bottle into Streeter's hands.

"This here is my wife," Streeter said. "Her name is Patty."

Leeman nodded his head, and looked like she was a surprise, and Streeter wondered how long since Leeman had eaten a meal in somebody's house, cooked by a wife.

After they had finished the steaks and mashed potatoes and spinach and cauliflower under some yellow sauce, Streeter and Leeman sat around the living room while Patty stacked the dishes in the dishwasher, and Streeter began to wonder if he had made a mistake with this invitation. Leeman wouldn't talk. Streeter would say something about the work, and Leeman would nod his head, and then they would sit in silence another couple of minutes, until Patty came in with a tray and three whiskey glasses of crème de menthe.

"What's it like?" she asked, looking at Leeman once they were all settled and through the first sip. Patty was sitting across from them on a footstool, and all at once Streeter wished she would pull down her skirt. Her reddish hair was curled tight around her head that summer, and she was wearing a plain white blouse that was tight around her breasts, and Leeman was looking at her in a curious way as he turned the glass of crème de menthe in his hands. Finally he shook his head like he didn't understand.

"Flying so close to the ground," Patty said. "I'd like to see what it was like." She scooted forward on the stool. "I mean there must be a moment," she went on, "when you settle down to the field and it looks like it would come right up around you, and you've got to stop yourself from sinking. I've been trying to imagine it."

"I guess you don't think much about it," Leeman said.

"Seems like a swing," Patty said. "You go down, but

you know you can never go so low, you can never really touch even when it seems like you will."

"Never thought about it that way."

Patty went on like she was excited, twisting on the stool and leaning forward with that glass held in both her hands, and pretty soon trying to talk Leeman into giving her a ride in the Steerman. Her skirt had worked higher, and Streeter was thinking he ought to break this up when Leeman said, "Tomorrow, when the breeze comes up."

"You get out there," Leeman said, "and I'll give you a ride." Then he looked to Streeter to see if it was all right and swallowed the last of his drink and stood up.

"Sun comes early," he said, and then he was out the door and heading toward his pickup. Patty was in the kitchen washing the drink glasses when Streeter looked around from the doorway. After that they argued a little, and she made it up to him in bed like they hadn't done in months. She surprised Streeter that night, like she would do every so often, and he lay awake when she was sleeping and knew it was a good thing she wanted to get out and do something.

The breeze came early the next day, and by eleven o'clock Streeter had Patty up on the gravel roadway through the brush Leeman had been using as a landing strip. Leeman was pumping fuel into his aircraft from the barrels in the back of his pickup with an old hand-crank pump, and Patty was biting at her lower lip as she watched. Remembering that morning, Streeter would think he had never felt so good with Patty since they were married children as he boosted her onto the wing and held her hand to steady her as she climbed over into the cockpit.

"Don't dump her out," Streeter shouted, and Leeman

smiled. Patty was wearing a Levi's jacket of Streeter's with the sleeves turned up a couple of rolls, and her hair was tied down with a silk bandanna. As she waved over the sides of the open cockpit Streeter thought she looked like some girl he might have dreamed about years before and could have known if they hadn't got married at eighteen.

Dust blew and the engine roared, and Streeter stood back as the Steerman bounced along and then lifted from the gravel roadway, Streeter watching until they turned low over the rolling sand hills and dropped from sight against the sun, and he thought about Patty frightened and felt sorry for her because she would be angry with herself when this was over, and say she should have known better, and he couldn't blame her for wanting to try something. Streeter ducked his head in the wind, which was coming in gusts from the southwest, like it did sometimes in early summer, and sat in the pickup and nipped on another little pint of Old Crow.

The Steerman was gone longer than he had guessed, and he wondered if the wind meant rain. Late-spring storms would most often come riding a blow like this, the country dry and already blowing dust one minute and then moist the next morning, the tilled soil dark and the sage softened and green under the soft rain.

Streeter had sipped at the whiskey four or five times when the Steerman returned, skimming low over the brush and then rising slightly and wheeling in the sky and dropping to the gravel roadway, touching down and bouncing slightly and then braking abruptly before taxiing toward Streeter, where he stood beside his pickup.

The prop-wash was still blowing dust behind them when Patty leaned forward from behind the pilot's seat and shouted something in Leeman's ear, gesturing at Streeter and then repeating whatever it was until Leeman shook his head and waved Streeter toward them. Leeman pulled his goggles up over his old leather helmet and grinned.

"Piggyback," he shouted over the dull noise of the idling engine, gesturing toward the cockpit where Patty was crouching behind the surprisingly small and cramped pilot's seat, her knees on a grease-stained sofa cushion. There were no safety straps for the rider, nothing to keep you in but gravity and your grasp on the tubing around the cockpit. Streeter thought what the hell and crawled awkwardly in behind her, and wedged himself, hunched forward with his arms around her and hands clamped to the cockpit edge.

Leeman revved the engine, dust and wind stinging around them, and the Steerman bumped and hurtled forward, rising as the sound diminished and they were skimming out over the sage flatlands before dropping over the rim along the north side of the valley swamps and down over the hayland meadows, lifting and falling over the sloughs and running sometimes only eight or ten feet off the ground, rising away from their shadow to flow over the banks of willow and wild rose along the fence lines and then falling so slightly again, until they were at the highway and lifting and nosing toward the sun and turning as they ascended over the roadside string of Lombardy poplar and falling into the turn as Streeter knew he was going to be sick.

The familiar fields and patterns were foreign and swept to a lost featureless blurring, like the sea under a green summer evening as the tipping horizon fell sideways in a long jerking sweep, and the warm bourbon came into Streeter's mouth as he managed to turn and twist himself, straining against the solid bulk of his wife as the horizon went on revolving, and then the vomit was gone, just that quick, in a long spew lost in the wind, and he was hunched there half out of the cockpit with Patty looking back to him and grinning as he wiped at his mouth. The Steerman began to lift and throttle into another steeply banking turn as Patty ducked to huddle her head against the back of Leeman's seat, her expression in the quick glance Streeter caught not so much sickened as haggard, as if watching him had turned her old while he fought to keep from falling.

A week later it did rain, and the work was stopped with maybe four or five hours to go. After breakfasting with his crew in the bunkhouse, Streeter turned them loose for the day and went home to crawl into bed with Patty, the bedroom door locked against the children, who were playing in the living room. It was almost noon when Streeter left the house again, and he took the children with him, a little boy and little girl, maybe four or five at the time, standing in the pickup seat beside him and keeping quiet and being good, as if awed by this special favor as Streeter drove the muddy meadow roads for an hour or so, checking his irrigation water, the wipers sweeping at the windshield and Streeter drawn to sadness with himself that left him surprised when he came home to find Leeman's pickup with the crushed tailgate parked in front of the house.

Patty opened the door as the children came running through the rain, and Leeman was sitting in the living room with a half-empty beer in his hand. Patty seated herself on the hassock stool again, sitting there hunched forward studying her hands, and nobody saying anything. After a slight hesitation, Leeman lifted his beer to Streeter as though in salute. "I ain't going to finish," he said.

Which was putting Streeter in a bind, and Streeter told him so. "Who the hell am I going to get?" Streeter asked. "You got any ideas?"

"Not a one," Leeman said. "I'm sorry about that, but I'm pulling out." He looked away from Streeter, and shifted his feet a little, and finished the beer.

"You know what I wish?" Patty said. "I wish I could just go off like that. I really do, for the rest of my life."

"She says she does," Leeman said. "But she don't."

There was a little quiet, and then Leeman got to his feet. "I'll be seeing you," he said. "Maybe you could write my check."

"My privilege," Streeter said, and he took out his personal checkbook, and looked to Patty for a pen. She sat looking back to him like he was gone crazy if he expected her to fetch him anything. "Need something to write with," Streeter said, and there was no sense to the anger in her eyes as she sat unmoving, the three of them locked there in place until Leeman fished in his shirt pocket and came out with an old giveaway ballpoint. "Try this," he said.

"Just round it off," Leeman said, "at five thousand."

"Since I'm leaving you early," Leeman said, and he folded the yellow check into his shirt pocket, clipped the ballpoint there, and was out the door.

"I could have gone, I wish I could," Patty said. "With him. I would have made him get me an Airstream trailer, and I would have gone, easy."

Streeter was running his fingers back and forth on the smooth hardwood of the mantel above his fireplace, just feeling the slight texture of the wood he had sanded and varnished so many years before. "How come?" he said.

"I could have asked him," she said. "He might have done it."

"Sounds to me like you did." This wasn't anything Streeter could imagine with any ease, and after one last swipe along the mantel where Patty polished away the dust every day, he slipped his hands flat into his back pockets and asked what this was getting at. "I don't think this is making any sense," he said.

Patty just sat there and shook her head like she was about to cry while the rain streaked the windows, and Streeter walked to the kitchen and back, and then they heard the crackling roar of the Steerman from where it was parked over by the highway and listened as it was climbing through the rain and turning and leaving until the dull throb of it was gone.

"It's nothing to do with flying," Patty said, looking up to Streeter and no longer fighting back her tears. "He just understood what things were worth."

There was no sensible answer. "Sounds to me like he turned you down," Streeter said, and the bottom of what he knew of himself was falling away, because it was true, for sure, and he walked out and spent the next eleven days sleeping down at the bunkhouse under the old blankets and heavy tarp from his hunting-camp bedroll, until one night he was drunk and went up to the house, and Patty shrieked at him for a fool, which seemed correct when he thought about it, and they ended up in bed.

The next morning was silent and they began a wary series of days in which nothing more was ever explained while the motions of their lives began to reassert themselves, and they slowly came together again as if nothing had ever happened, and maybe it hadn't, Streeter could never bring himself to really ask. In the end it wasn't so bad and Streeter could lie there in their bedroom before sleep and in the eye of his imagination see someone who might be her with another man, just the man's white and muscular naked back, and feel them trembling, and try again to understand that transgressions and betrayals and violations of trust and guilt had nothing to do with anything that was his life while the children grew and the grass grew back where the brush had been killed by chemicals, and Patty learned to laugh and study him like only another problem in her life that would never be solved on the ground.

Ben Alton remembered years in terms of winter. Summers all ran together, each like the last, heat and baled hay and dust. "That was '59," he'd say. "The year I wintered in California." He'd be remembering manure-slick alleys of a feedlot outside Manteca, a flat horizon and constant rain.

Or flood years. "March of '64, when the levees went." Or open winters. "We fed cattle the whole of February in our shirtsleeves. For Old Man Swarthout." And then he'd be sad. "One week Art helped. We was done every day by noon and drunk by three." Sad because Art was his stepbrother and dead, and because there'd been nothing but hate between them when Art was killed.

Ben and Art fought only once, when they were thirteen. Ben's father, Corrie Alton, moved in with Art's old lady on her dryland place in the hills north of Davanero, and the boys bunked together in a back room. The house was surrounded by a fenced dirt yard where turkeys picked, shaded by three withering peach trees; and the room they shared was furnished with two steel-frame cots and a row of nails where they hung what extra clothing they owned. The first night, while the old people were drinking in town, the boys fought. Ben took a flattened nose and chipped tooth against one of the cot frames and was satisfied and didn't try again.

The next year Art's mother sold the place for money

to drink on, and when that was gone Ben's old man pulled out, heading for Shafter, down out of Bakersfield, going to see friends and work a season in the spuds. Corrie never came back or sent word, so the next spring the boys took a job setting siphons for an onion farmer, doing the muddy and exhausting work of one man, supporting themselves and Art's mother. She died the spring they were seventeen; and Art began to talk about getting out of town, fighting in the ring, being somebody.

So he ran every night, and during the day he and Ben stacked alfalfa bales, always making their thousand a day, twenty bucks apiece, and then in the fall Art went to Portland and worked out in a gym each afternoon, learning to fight, and spent his evenings swimming at the YMCA or watching movies. Early in the winter he began to get some fights; and for at least the first year he didn't lose. People began to know his name in places like Salem and Yakima and Klamath Falls.

He fought at home only once, a January night in the Peterson barn on the edge of town, snow falling steadily. The barn warmed slowly, losing its odor of harness leather and rotting hay; and under a circle of lights that illuminated the fighters in a blue glare, country people smoked and bet and drank. Circling a sweating and tiring Mexican boy, Art tapped his gloves and brushed back his thin blond hair with a quick forearm, sure and quiet. Then he moved under an overhand right, ducking in a quick new way he must have learned in Portland; and then he was inside, forcing, and flat on his feet, grunting as he followed each short chop with his body. The Mexican backed against one of the rough juniper posts supporting the ring, covered his face, gloves fumbling together as he began sinking and twisting, knees folding;

and it ended with the Mexican sprawled and cut beneath one eye, bleeding from the nose, and Art in his corner, breathing easily while he flexed and shook his arms as if he weren't loose yet. Art spit the white mouthpiece onto the wet, gray canvas and ducked away under the ropes.

That night, Ben sat in the top row of the little grandstand and watched two men drag the other fighter out of the ring and attempt to revive him by pouring water over his head. Ben hugged his knees and watched the crowd settle and heard the silence while everybody watched. Finally the Mexican boy shook his head and stood up, and the crowd moved in a great sigh.

The next summer Art showed up with Clara, brought her back with him from a string of fights in California. It was an August afternoon, dead hot in the valley hayfields, and dust rose in long spirals from the field ahead where five balers were circling slowly, eating windrows of loose hay and leaving endless and uniform strings of bales. Ben was working the stack, unloading trucks, sweating through his pants every day before noon, shirtless and peeling.

The lemon-colored Buick convertible came across the stubble, bouncing and wheeling hard, just ahead of its own dust, and stopped twenty or thirty yards from the stack. Art jumped out holding a can of beer over his head. The girl stood beside the convertible in the dusty alfalfa stubble and squinted into the glaring light, moist and sleepy looking. She was maybe twenty, and her sleeveless white blouse was wrinkled from sleeping in the car and sweat-gray beneath the arms. But she was blond and tan and direct in the 100-degree heat of the afternoon. "Ain't she something?" Art said. "She's a kind of prize I brought home." He laughed and slapped her on the butt.

"Hello, Ben," she said. "Art told me about you." They

drank a can of beer, iced and metallic tasting, and Art talked about the fighting in California, Fresno, and Tracy, and while he talked he ran his fingers slowly up and down Clara's bare arm. Ben crouched in the shade of the convertible with his beer and tried not to watch the girl. That night he lay awake and thought about her, and everything about that meeting seemed too large and real, like some memory of childhood.

Anyway, she was living and traveling with Art. Then the fall he was twenty-five, fighting in Seattle, Art broke his right hand in a way that couldn't be fixed and married Clara and came home to live, driving a logging truck in the summer and drinking in the bars and drawing his unemployment through the winters, letting Clara work as a barmaid when they were broke. The years got away until one afternoon in a tavern called The Tarpaper Shack, when Ben and Art were thirty-one. Art was sitting with a girl named Marie, and when Ben came in and wandered over to the booth she surprised him by being quiet and nice, with brown eyes and dark hair, not the kind Art ran with on his drunks; and by the end of the summer Marie and Ben were engaged.

Which caused no trouble until Christmas. The stores were open late, but the streets with their decorations were deserted, looking like a carnival at four in the morning, lighted and ready to tear down and move.

"You gonna marry that pig?" Art said. Art was drunk. The barkeeper, a woman called Virgie, was leaning on the counter.

"I guess I am," Ben said. "But don't sweat it." Then he noticed Virgie looking past them to the far corner of the vaulted room. A worn row of booths ran there, beyond the lighted shuffleboard table and bowling machine.

Above the last booth he saw the shadowed back of Clara's head. Just the yellow hair and yet certainly her. Art was grinning.

"You see her," he said talking to Ben. "She's got a problem. She ain't getting any."

Ben finished the beer and eased the glass back to the wooden counter, wishing he could leave, wanting no more of their trouble. Clara was leaning back, eyes closed and the table in front of her empty except for her clasped hands. She didn't move or look as he approached.

"Hello, Clara," he said. And when she opened her eyes it was the same, like herons over the valley swamps, white against green. Even tired she looked good. "All right if I sit?" he asked. "You want a beer?"

She sipped from his, taking the glass without speaking, touching his hand with her hand, then smiling and licking the froth from her lips. "Okay," she said, and he ordered another glass and sat down beside her.

"How you been?" he said. "All right?"

"You know," she said, looking sideways at him, never glancing toward Art. "You got a pretty good idea how I been." Then she smiled. "I hear you're getting married."

"Just because you're tied up," he said, and she grinned again, more like her old self now. "I mean it," he said. "Guess I ought to tell you once."

"Don't," she said. "For Christ sake. Not with that bastard over there laughing." She drank a little more of the beer. "I mean it," she said, after a moment. "Leave me alone."

Ben picked up his empty glass and walked toward the bar, turning the glass in his hand and feeling how it fit his grasp. He stood looking at the back of Art's head, the thin hair, fine and blond; and then he wrapped the glass in his fist and smashed it into the hollow of Art's neck, shattering the glass and driving Art's face into the counter. Then he ran, crashing out the door and onto the sidewalk.

His hand was cut and bleeding. He picked glass from his palm and wrapped his hand in his handkerchief as he walked, looking in the store windows, bright and lighted for Christmas.

Clara left for Sacramento that night, lived there with her father, worked in a factory southeast of town, making airplane parts and taking care of the old man, not coming back until he died. Sometimes Ben wondered if she would have come back anyway, even if the old man hadn't died. Maybe she's just been waiting for Art to come after her. And then one day on the street he asked, "You and Art going back together?" just hoping he could get her to talk awhile.

"I guess not," she said. "That's what he told me."

"I'm sorry," Ben said. And he was.

"I came back because I wanted," she said. "Guess I lived here too long."

That spring Ben and Marie were married and began living out of town, on a place her father owned; and the next fall his father was killed, crushed under a hillside combine in Washington, just north of Walla Walla, drunk and asleep at the leveling wheel, dead when they dug him out. And then the summer Art and Ben turned thirty-four Marie got pregnant and that winter Art was killed, shot in the back of the head by a girl named Stephanie Rudd, a thin red-haired girl just out of high school and, so people said, knocked up a little. Art was on the end stool in The Tarpaper Shack, his usual place, when the girl entered quietly and shot before anyone noticed. He was dead when he hit the floor, face destroyed, blood spattered over the mirror and glasses behind the bar. And all the time music he'd punched was playing on the jukebox. *Trailer for sale or rent*; and *I can't stop loving you*; and, *Time to bum again*; and, *That's what you get for loving me*: Roger Miller, Ray Charles, Waylon Jennings.

Ben awakened the night of the shooting and heard Marie on the phone, felt her shake him awake in the dim light of the bedroom. She seemed enormously frightened and continued to shake him, as if to awaken herself. She was eight months pregnant.

"He's dead." She spoke softly, seeming terrified, as if some idea she feared had been at last confirmed. "He never had a chance," she said.

"He had plenty." Ben sat up and put his arm around her, forced from his shock.

"They never gave him anything." She bent over and began to cry.

Later, it was nearly morning, after coffee and cigarettes, when Marie gave up and went to bed; Ben sat alone at the kitchen table. "Afraid of everything," Art had said. "That's how they are. Every stinking one."

Ben saw Art drunk and talking like he was ready for anything, actually involved with nothing except for a string of girls like the one who shot him. And then, some-how, the idea of Art and Marie got hold of Ben. It came from the way she had cried and carried on about Art. There was something wrong. Sitting there at the table, feeling the knowledge seep around his defenses, Ben knew what it was. He got up from the chair.

She was in the bedroom, curled under the blankets, crying softly. "What is it?" he asked. "There's something going on." She didn't open her eyes, but the crying seemed to slow a little. Ben waited, standing beside the bed, looking down, all the time wondering, as he became more sure, if it had happened in this bed, and all the time knowing it made no difference where it happened. And it was her fault. Not any fault of Art's. Art was what he was. She could have stopped him. Ben's hands felt strange, as if there was something to be done he couldn't recognize. He asked again, hearing his voice harsh and strained. "What is it, Marie?"

She didn't answer. He forced her onto her back and held her there, waiting for her to open her eyes while she struggled silently, twisting her upper body against his grip. His fingers sank into her shoulder and his wrist trembled. They remained like that, forcing against each other. Then she relaxed and opened her eyes. "What is it?" he asked again. "It was something between you and Art, wasn't it?"

Her eyes were changed, shielded. She shook her head. "No," she said. "No."

"He was screwing you, wasn't he? Is it his kid?"

"It was a long time ago," she said.

"My ass." He let go of her shoulder. "That's why you're so tore up. Because you ain't getting any more from him." He walked around the bed, unable for some reason, because of what he was left with, to ask her if it happened here, in this bed. "Isn't that right?" he said. "How come you married me? He turn you down?"

"Because I was afraid of him. I didn't want him. He was just fooling. I wanted you, not him."

Ben slapped her, and she curled quickly again, her hands pressed to her mouth, crying, shoulders hunching. He made her face him. "You ain't getting away," he said. "So I was a nice tame dog, and you took me."

"You'll hurt the baby."

"His goddamned baby!"

"It all broke off when I met you," she said. "He told me to go ahead, that you'd be good to me." It had surprised him when they met that she was with Art, but somehow he'd never until now gotten the idea they had anything going on. "It was only a few times after I knew you," she said. "He begged me."

"So I got stuck with the leavings." He cursed her again, at the same time listening to at least a little of what she said. "He begged me." That was sad. Remembering Art those last years, after he came home to stay, Ben believed her.

"So he dumped you off onto me," Ben said. "I wish I could thank him."

"It wasn't like that. He loved you. He said for me to marry you and be happy."

"So you did. And I was stupid enough to go for it."

"He was a little boy. It was fun, but he was a little boy."

"I'm happy," Art said, "things worked out so nice for you." She shook her head and didn't answer. Ben wondered what he should do. It was as if he had never been married, had been right in always imagining his life as single. He'd watched his friends settle, seen their kids start to grow up, and it had seemed those were things he was not entitled to, that he was going to grow old in a habit of taverns, rented rooms, separate from the married world. And now he was still there, outside. And she'd kept it all a secret. "You stinking pig," he said slowly.

"Ben, it was a long time ago. Ben."

He was tired and his work was waiting. Maybe it was a long time ago and maybe it wasn't. He left her there crying while he dressed to go out and feed her father's cattle.

In the afternoon she had the house picked up and a

meal waiting. She watched while he ate, but they didn't talk. He asked if she wanted to go to the funeral, and she said no and that was all. When he was drinking his coffee, calm now, and so tired his chest ached, he started thinking about Clara. He wondered if she'd known. Wouldn't have made any difference, he thought. Not after everything else.

Three days later, heading for the burial, he was alone and hunched against the wheel, driving through new snow that softly drifted across the highway. His fingers were numb, the broken cracks in the rough calluses ingrained with black. A tire chain ticked a fender, but he kept going. He'd gone out at daylight to feed, a mandatory job that had to be done every day of winter, regardless of other obligations. The rust-streaked Chevrolet swayed on the rutted ice beneath the snow. The steady and lumbering gait of the team he fed with, two massive frost-coated Belgian geldings, the creaking oceanic motion of the hay wagon, was still with him, more real than this.

The Derrick County cemetery was just below the road, almost five miles short of town. They were going to bury Art in the area reserved for charity burials, away from the lanes of Lombardy poplars and old-time lilacs. By dark the grave would be covered with snow. Ben parked and got out, and went over to look down in the hole. Far away in town, the bells of the Catholic church were faintly tolling. Ben stood a moment, then started back toward the car. He sat in the front seat with his hands cupped in his crotch, warming them. After a time, he backed slowly out of the graveyard.

Davanero was on the east side of the valley, scattered houses hung with ice, windows sealed against wind by tacked-on plastic sheeting. The still smoke of house fires rose straight up. Ben drove between lots heaped with snow-covered junk, past shacks with open, hanging doors where drifters lived in summer, into the center of town. The stores were open and a few people moved toward the coffee shops. He felt cut away from everything, as if this were an island in the center of winter.

The OPEN sign hung in the front window of The Tarpaper Shack. Ben wondered if Clara was tending bar and if she intended to go to the funeral. He parked and walked slowly through the snow to the door. The church bells were louder, close and direct now. Inside, the tavern was dark and barn-like, empty except for Clara, who was washing glasses in a metal sink. Ben went to the far end, where Art always sat, and eased onto a stool. "I'd take a shot," he said. "A double. Take one yourself."

"I'm closing up," she said. "So there's no use hanging around." She stayed at the sink and continued to wash glasses.

"You going to the funeral?" Ben said.

"I'm closing up." Her hands were still in the water. "I guess you need a drink," she said. "Go lock the door."

She was sitting in one of the booths when he got back. "You ain't going to the funeral?" he asked again.

"What good is that?"

"I guess you feel pretty bad."

"I guess." She drank quietly. "I would have took anything off him. Any damned thing. And that stupid bitch kills him. I would have given anything for his kid."

Ben finished his whiskey, and Clara took his glass and went for some more. "To hell with their goddamned funeral," he said.

Clara played some music on the jukebox, slow country stuff; and they danced staggering against the stools and the shuffleboard table, holding each other. She pushed him away after a few songs. "If you ain't one hell of a dancer," she said. "Art was a pretty dancer." She sat down in the booth and put an arm on the table and then lay her head alongside it, facing the wall. "Goddamn," she said. "I could cry. I ain't cried since I was a little girl," she said. "Not since then. Not since I was a little girl."

Ben wandered around the barroom, carrying his drink. He called his wife on the telephone. "You bet your sweet ass I'm drunk," he shoulted when she answered, then hung up.

"Ain't you some hero," Clara said. She drank what whiskey was left in her glass. "You're nothing," she said. "Absolutely nothing."

Outside, the bells had stopped. Nothing. That was what he felt like. Nothing. Like his hands were without strength to steer the car. He sat awhile in the front seat, then drove to the jail, a gray brick building with heavy wire mesh over the windows. The deputy, a small bald man in a gray uniform, sat behind a desk in the center of the main room, coffee cup beside him. He smiled when he saw Ben, but he didn't say anything.

"How's chances of seeing that girl?" Ben asked. He didn't know why he'd come. It was just some idea that because she'd hated Art enough to kill him, because of that, maybe she understood and could tell him, Ben, why he wasn't nothing. He knew, even while he spoke, that it was a stupid, drunk idea.

"Okay," the deputy said, after a minute. "Come on. I guess you got a right."

They went through two locked doors, back into a large cinder-block room without any windows. Light came from a long fluorescent tube overhead. Two cells were separated by steel bars six inches apart. The room was warm. The girl was sitting on a cot in the left-hand cell, legs crossed, with red hair straight down over her shoulders and wearing a wrinkled blue smock without any pockets. She was looking at her hands, which were folded in her lap. "What now?" she said when she looked up. Her voice was surprisingly loud.

"Ben wanted to see you," the deputy said.

"Like a zoo, ain't it." The girl grinned and raised and lowered her shoulders.

"And you're not one bit sorry?" Ben said. "Just a little bit sorry for what you did?"

"Not one bit," the girl said. "I've had plenty of time to think about that. I'm not. I'm happy. I feel good."

"He wasn't no bad man," Ben said. "Not really. He never really was."

"He sure as hell wasn't Winston Churchill. He never even *tried* to make me happy." She put her hands in her lap.

"I don't see it," Ben said. "No way I can see you're right. He wasn't that bad."

"The thing I liked about him," she said, "was that he was old enough. He was like you. He was old enough to do anything. He could have been nice if he'd wanted."

The deputy laughed.

"I felt so bad before," the girl said, "killing him was easy. The only thing I feel bad about is that I never got down into him and made him crawl around. That's the only thing. I'm sorry about that, but that's all."

"He didn't owe you nothing," Ben said.

The girl looked at the deputy. "Make him leave," she said.

Ben drove slowly home in the falling snow. He could only see blurred outlines of the trees on either side of the lane that led to his house. He parked the car, kicked the snow from his boots, and went inside the house. Marie was in the bedroom, sleeping. The dim room was gray and cold, the bed a rumpled island. Marie was on her back, her stomach a mound beneath the blankets. Her mouth gaped a little.

After he got out of his clothes, Ben sat on the edge of the bed. Marie sighed in her sleep and moved a little, but she didn't waken. Ben reached to touch her shoulder and then stopped. Her eyelids flickered open. "Come on," she said. "Get under the covers."

"In a minute," Ben said. He went back out to the kitchen and smoked a cigarette. Then he went back into the bedroon and crawled in beside her and put his hand on her belly, hoping to feel the baby move. He remembered a warm, shirtsleeve day in February, working with Art, hurrying while they fed a final load of bales to the cattle that trailed behind, eager to get to town, noon sun glaring off wind-glazed fields of snow.

THE WATERFOWL TREE

They ran into snow almost two hours before reaching the valley, the storm at twilight whipping in gusts across the narrow asphalt. The station wagon moved slowly through the oncoming darkness.

"A long haul," his father said. "Eva will be wondering."

The boy, tall and seventeen, his hands behind his neck, watched out the glazed and crusted side window at the indeterminate light. This mention of the woman could be a signal, some special beginning.

"Is she pretty?" he asked.

"Pretty enough for me. And that's pretty enough."

The man laughed and kept his eyes on the road. He was massive, a widower in his late fifties. "I've got too old for worrying about pretty," he said. "All I want is gentle. When that's all you want, you got to be getting old."

In a little while, the man said, "I remember hunting when I was a kid. It was different then, more birds for one thing, and you had to kill something with every shot."

"How do you mean?" the boy asked.

"We were meat hunters. You spent money for shells, you brought home meat. I saw Teddy Spandau die on that account. Went off into open water chest deep, just trying to get some birds he shot. Cramped up and drowned. We hauled a boat down and fished him out that afternoon."

29

The snow began to thin and the man pushed the car faster and concentrated on his driving.

"It was like this then," he said. "Snowing, and ice a foot thick and below zero all day."

The boy wished his father would go on talking about these faraway and unsuspected things. But the man, long estranged from this remote and misted valley of his childhood, sat hunched over the wheel, absorbed in the road and grimacing.

"I guess it was different in those days," the boy said, wanting his father to keep talking.

"Quite a bit different," the man answered. "A different life altogether."

After this they drove in silence. It was completely dark when they came out of the storm, driving through the last drifting flakes into the light of a full moon and an intense and still cold that made the new snow crystallize and occasionally sparkle in the headlights.

"Freeze solid by morning," the man said. "Be some new birds coming in."

He stopped the car and switched off the headlights.

"Look there," he said, pointing.

The boy cranked down his window and looked across the distorted landscape of snow, blue and subdued in the moonlight. Far away he saw a high ridge shadowed in darkness.

"That's the rim," his father said. "We'll be home directly."

The boy looked again at the black fault. How could this be home, this place under that looming wall?

"All my life," the man said, "in strange places, I've caught myself looking up and expecting to see that rim."

The long attic room, unfinished, raftered under the peak roof, filled with soft darkness, illuminated by blue softness where moonlight shone through windows on either end. On the floor and inward sloping east wall he could see light reflected up from downstairs. The boy lay in the bundled warmth of a mummy bag on an iron cot and watched the light, imagined that he could see it slowly climb the wall as the moon dropped. The cold in this shed-like room above the barn was complete and still and frosted his breath when he moved.

"You're young and tough," his father had said. "You draw the outdoor room."

They'd unloaded the boy's suitcase and the new gear quickly in the darkness, tried to be quiet because the house across the road was completely dark. Then his father went ahead with a flashlight and they carried the gear up an old flight of stairs at the side of the barn and pushed through the ancient hanging door that opened into this long, barren room. After unrolling the sleeping bag on the cot, his father gripped him by the shoulder and shone the light in his face.

"You'll be warm inside the bag," the man said. "Take your coat in with you and sleep with your clothes on. That way they won't be frozen in the morning. Stick the boots under you. We'll get you up for breakfast."

Then he turned and took the light and left the boy standing in the cold. What would greet his father in that dark house across the road? They'd come upon the place after rounding a curve in the gravel road that crossed the upper part of the valley. A bunch of trees and a house and a barn and some corrals; just that in the midst of unending fields of fenced snow.

The boots made a comforting hump and the boy curled around them and tried to warm himself. Suddenly he was frantic and wished he were back in his bed at school, enduring the vacation, trying to guess tomorrow's movie.

"Goddamn," he said, clenching and shaking. "Damn, dirty son of a bitch."

But the warmth came and with it a quiet numbness. He felt himself drift and then he slept, surprised that he was not going to lie awake and search for a sense of how it would be in the morning.

And now, just as quickly, he was awake and watching the slow light on the far wall. Then he recognized, almost unnoticed among his thoughts, an ancient crying. Coyotes. He smiled and huddled deep in his warmth, secure against the night. The calls came fine and clear, and he struggled to get an arm out of the warmth. He looked at the illuminated face of his watch. It was almost three o'clock.

The wailing stopped and there was silence.

Geese were flying. He could hear, far away, but still clear and distinct, their wandering call. He felt himself slipping again into peaceful sleep. Then the coyotes began a long undulating wail and small yipping. He rested his head on his arm and slept, lulled by their noise and a small rhythm of his own.

A hand shook him, gently and firmly, and for a moment he was elsewhere and lost, then he was awake and remembering. He pushed up from the warmth of the sleeping bag and looked out at the morning, at the smile of this strange woman and the frosted windows, and the rough shingle and rafter roof. His breath swirled softly in the cold morning air. He smiled at the woman and stretched his arms. The woman stood next to his bed, leaning over, one hand touching him through the layers of the sleeping bag.

"Welcome," she said. "On the coldest day in a thousand years."

Really nothing but a fuzzy-headed woman. She was bundled in hunting clothes and wore a down cap tied under her chin with fringes and curls of hair protruding. Not the woman he'd expected. The face was heavier and older than he would have imagined, and he suddenly understood that his father was almost an old man.

"You must be Eva."

"The same," she said. "The famous Eva. Come on, breakfast is almost ready."

"I can't." He grinned, surprised at her easiness, taken in spite of himself. "I don't have any pants on."

"Come on. I won't look if I can help myself." She pulled on his arm and grinned.

He scrambled out of bed and was shocked at the cold. He jumped in dismay when she grabbed one of his bare ankles with her cold hands. He escaped and she dropped the mittens she had tucked under one arm and began rummaging in the bed, fishing in the warm darkness, finally pulling out his pants and coat while he wrapped his arms around himself and watched. "Get 'em on," she said.

The area between the house and the barn was ankle deep in new snow and marked only by the boot tracks of the night before and her footprints of this morning. The trees around the house were heaped with ice and snow. He had to squint against the glare.

The house was rough and worn and old, without any rugs to cover the plank floor and with homemade wooden chairs and a long table with benches on either side. The boy stood in the doorway and felt with pleasure the shock of warm air that softened his face. In one corner of this main room was a big woodstove with chopped wood and kindling in a box beside it. His father sat on a stool beside the stove, filling shell belts. Open shell boxes were scattered around him on the floor.

"Come on in," the man said. "Close the door. Charlie will have breakfast on in a minute."

Through an open doorway on the far side of the room came the reflection of morning sunlight. Through the doorway he could see another smaller man working over a wood-burning cook stove. The woman began pulling off her cap and coat, piling them on the far end of the table. No one, not even the woman, paid attention to the water and melting ice on the floor.

"Holy smokes," the woman said, brushing her hair back and tucking her shirt in her pants. "It's so damned cold out there he could have froze."

"Make you tough, won't it, boy?" His father looked up at him.

"It wasn't bad," the boy said. "I stayed warm."

"That's the spirit." The man stood up, dropping the finished shell belts from his lap to the floor. "Come on."

The boy followed him into the next room where the other man was tending a frying pan full of eggs and another pan with bacon. "This is Charlie Anderson," his father said. "Me and Charlie are hunting partners. From the old days."

Charlie turned and shook hands with the boy. "Glad to have you, son," he said. "Eat in a minute." Charlie nodded and went back to his cooking.

"Come here." His father, massive in boots and khaki hunting gear, walked to the far end of the kitchen and opened a door to the outside. The boy followed him out, and the cold was at him again, hard and stiff.

"Look at that," his father said. Behind the house was a small orchard of six or seven trees. The tree nearest the house, gnarled and holding stiff winter limbs toward the thin sky, was hung with dead geese and ducks. They were in bunches of a dozen or more, strung together on short pieces of rope and suspended from heavy nails driven into limbs, crusted with ice and frozen and absolutely still, frosted and sparkling in the light.

"Deep freeze," the man said. "We hung them like that when we were kids."

The boy supposed that he should say something to please his father but was not sure what that would be. He turned away from the tree and looked to the west where the winter rim he had seen in the moonlight rose high over the far edge of the valley. Through the still air he could define individual trees among the groves of juniper along its upper edge. He heard the geese calling again and looked to see them flying, distant and wavering, and remembered the night before. "They sound so far away," he said.

"We'll get after them," his father said. "As soon as we eat."

The boy turned and looked again at the tree, hung with dead birds. He was unable to feel anything beyond his own chill.

"We hung them there when I was a kid," his father said. "A man named Basston owned this place, and my old man would bring me down here to help out on the weekends. There'd be a crowd all season. Guys from the city. Basston died. The guys stopped coming. Let's eat."

The boy watched his father turn and go in, surprised at the life that had been his father's. Maybe that's why he brought me here, he thought. To let me see what he was.

"Coming," he said.

The boy huddled lower in the blind of tules and reeds and wished the birds would hurry and come again. He and his father sat hidden only a few yards from a small patch of open water, on a neck of land in the tule swamps of the valley. They were alone and a long way from the warmth of the station wagon.

"I'll take you with me," the man said when they first spotted the birds. He pointed far off from where they were parked above the frozen swamp, and the boy saw them, milling and keeping a stired bit of water open and free of ice. A fantastic sight through the field glasses—thousands of ducks crowding in the water and great bunches of honkers and lesser Canadians walking the ice around them.

"Eva and Charlie can go over and wait at the decoys," his father said. "Give us two shots at them."

No one said anything, and after straightening the tangled gear in the back of the station wagon, the four of them walked off, two in each direction. The boy and his father walked in a long arc around the birds in order to come up on them from the sheltered land side and get as close as possible before they flushed. "Lots of time," his father said, after they'd walked a half mile or so. He was panting and sweating in the heavy gear. "Give Eva and Charlie time to get over to the decoys."

And their stalk was a good one. Between them, they had five greenhead Mallard drakes and two hens. "Pick the greenheads," his father whispered before they came up shooting. "Pick one each time before you shoot."

The geese had been too wise and flushed early, taking a few ducks with them, but the main flock of ducks was almost too easy, standing nearly still in the air during the long and suddenly clamorous second as they flushed, rising in waves, time to reload and shoot again before they were gone. The boy's first two shots had simply been pulled off into the rising mass. Then he remembered his father's words and aimed carefully and selectively.

After the first flush, the man and the boy dropped into the tules near the water's edge, leaving the dead birds on the ice. The thousands of ducks grouped and then turned in the distance and came back at them in long whirring masses, sensing something and veering off before getting into shooting range, but filling the air with the mounting rush of their wings. The boy, awed nearly to tears by the sight above him and the sound of the wings, sat concealed beside his father and was unable and unready to shoot again.

"Charlie and I used to hunt here when we were kids," the man said after a time, during a lull. "This is the real coming back. I remember waking in the spring when the birds were flying north. I could hear them from my bed, and I'd go out and stand on the knoll behind the house and watch them leave and hear them calling and smell the corrals and just look at the valley where it had turned green and then over at the rim where a little snow lay near the top. I guess those were the best days I ever lived." The man spoke softly, and the boy half-listened to him and sucked in his breath, waiting for the birds to come wheeling at them again, thinking the sound of their flight the most beautiful thing he had ever heard.

Then the birds stopped coming, and he and his father went out on the ice and gathered the dead ones, five beautiful greenheads and the two hens and carried them back to the hiding place. "The dead ones scared them off," his father said. "Now we'll have to wait awhile on the honkers."

And so they waited, the boy trying to be comfortable in his heavy clothing as he listened to his father.

"We used to haul the birds back to the house in a wagon. There was ten times as many in those days and lots of canvasbacks and redheads. You don't see those birds here anymore." The man moved quietly and easily around their nest, pulling reeds together over them until they were completely hidden.

"I remember one afternoon when the wind was blowing and the clouds were below the rim and we sat in one place, Charlie and me, fourteen years old I guess, and we shot up over a case of Basston's 12-gauge shells. The birds kept coming and we just kept shooting. We killed a hundred and fifty birds that one afternoon. It was almost night when we got back to camp and we hung those birds in the dark and Old Man Basston came out and we stood under that tree and he gave each of us a couple of drinks of the best bourbon whiskey on earth and sent us to bed like men. I guess that was the best day, the tops in my life."

Had everything been downhill since? The boy understood, or hoped that he did, why he was here, that his father was trying to make up, to present a view of life before the time had completely passed. Was this only for himself, he wondered? He listened to his father and thought of this woman, Eva, and the others and the different man his father had become to him in this place.

Eventually the geese came, very high and veered out in their great formations. They dropped and started to wheel when they saw the water.

The flocks seemed endless, long flights coming one before the next, circling and wheeling and dropping. "I'll tell you when," the man said. "Just lie quiet."

The first flight had landed and was calming itself in the water and on the edge of the ice when the next, under a larger flight of ducks, came directly over them, settled on stiff wings, fell directly toward the water, unconscious and intent. "Now," the man said, and they rose, waist deep in the tules, and shot three times each and dropped six birds easily, the huge black and white geese thudding on the ice.

"That's it," his father said. "Beautiful shooting. Enough for this day. Let's go. They'll be back."

The geese scattered and wheeled above them while they went out on the ice again and began to pick up the dead birds. They were heavy and beautiful birds and the boy twisted their necks the way his father did and felt sorry that they could not have lived and yet was glad that they were dead. They were trophies of this world, soft and heavy and dead birds.

"We'll sit around this afternoon and play some four-handed gin," his father said, after they had gathered the birds. "You ever play gin?"

"Sure," the boy said. "For pennies and buttons." They strung the ducks on a short piece of rope and the geese on another. "You carry the ducks," his father said. "I'll bring the geese. We'll go back across the ice."

It was a mile across to where the station wagon sat on a knoll. The going was slick and tricky with the new snow on the ice. The boy walked gingerly at first, then faster. Soon he was well out ahead of his father. The man came slowly and solidly, breathing heavily.

Far away the rim was a sharply defined edge. Between him and that high point, the boy watched the flocks of birds, some clearly visible against the flat sky, others almost indistinguishable against the snow-covered slopes.

From behind him he heard a distant, muffled cry.

He turned and saw that his father was gone, vanished from sight. Then the man reappeared on the surface of the snow, floundering in the water. The boy dropped the shotgun and the birds and ran toward his father.

While running he saw the man raise himself violently and wave, shout, then fall back again.

The cry, the boy understood, was a command to stay back; but he ran on, slipping and falling toward the hole in the ice. The man floundered through the chest-deep water, while the geese on their little rope floated beside him. The water steamed. The ice, incredibly, was soft and only a few inches thick.

The man waved him back and the boy stopped, yards short of the edge. He watched his father for some sign of what had happened, what to do.

The man stood quietly in the steaming and putrid water, gasping. He had been completely submerged and now the water was under his armpits. "Stay there," his father said, beginning to shake. "There's a hot spring and the ice is rotten."

"Let me rest a little," he said. "Then I'll try to work my way over to the solid ice."

The boy stood helpless. The edges of the broken and jagged water had begun to freeze again, solidifying as he watched. "Can you stand it?"

"It's not so bad here," the man said, composed now and shaking less, speaking quietly. "But it'll be cold out there."

Then the man began to move again, working slowly, pulling each leg out of the deep bottom mud and then moving forward another step. He made it almost to the edge of the ice and then stopped. "God Almighty," he said. "It's so goddamned cold."

And then the boy heard his father mutter something else, something subdued and private, and saw his face begin to collapse and draw into itself and grow distant. The man began to thrash and move forward in lunges, reaching toward the edge of the ice, fighting and gasping, moving toward the boy.

Then, his eyes on the boy, the man simply turned

onto his back, eyes rolling back and becoming blank. Then he sank, flailing his arms, the birds entangled in the rope going down with him. Then there was nothing but the water and some bubbling.

And then there were no bubbles, nothing but the dead geese floating quietly, their heads pulled under the surface by the rope that still encircled his father's body.

The boy heard again the distant honking of the geese and the whirring of wings as a pair of ducks came directly at him and suddenly swung away.

The boy turned and began to rush across the ice, scrambling and slipping, sometimes falling as he ran across the open ice toward the station wagon.

Back in the station wagon with the engine going and the heater turned on, he began to shake. He stretched out on the seat and fell out of himself like a stone into what might have been taken for sleep.

He awoke fully in the warm darkness of a completely strange and unknown room, wondering what place this was. And then, with terrible swiftness, he was again in the moment of the inexplicable thing that had happened— he saw his father's eyes rolling backward. He knew that it had happened, understood that this was one of the bedrooms in the strange house. He put his feet on the floor and was surprised to find himself in his underwear. A door slammed in another part of the house and he heard a voice, Eva's voice.

"I wonder if he's still sleeping?"

She appeared in the dim doorway.

"He's awake," she said over her shoulder.

She came into the room and turned on the light. Her hair was brushed away from her face and fell in waves to her shoulders. She looked younger, he thought, and somehow out of place here. He pulled the sheets over his bare legs.

"I'm all right now," he said. "Did they get him out?"

"He is out." The woman spoke formally and slowly, showing, the boy thought, that they were still really strangers, after all. "And now it is night. You slept a long time."

The boy turned away, beginning to cry, dissolving into the terror once more. The woman snapped off the light and came across the room to him. "Try to rest," she said, "I'm going to bed now."

"Your father loved this place," the woman said. "He told me it was the only surely happy place in his life. I'll be back in a minute," Eva said, and left the room.

The only surely happy place.

Presently the woman returned, wearing a brocade robe that reached the floor and with her hair pulled back and knotted behind her head. The boy turned and looked at her in the dim light, saw her drop the robe and pull back the covers on the other side of the bed and get under the covers, flinching when she touched the sheets. The boy started to get up.

"Stay and we'll talk," she said. She took him by the arm and pulled him toward her, and he was again surprised at the coldness of her hands.

"Why?" he said. "Why did it happen?" He began to cry again.

"His heart," she said. "He had been having trouble." The woman moved closer to him and put her arm around his shoulders. "I'm sorry," she said. "God," she said.

Presently he slept again, exhausted and calmed, slowly moving to huddle against the warmth of the woman. In the middle of the night he woke and felt the woman shuddering and crying beside him.

He woke to warmth and sunlight coming through the open doorway of the room. He was alone in the bed.

In the outer room the woman and Charlie Anderson were sitting quietly at the table. "Sit down," Charlie said. "I'll get you some food."

"Charlie doesn't trust my cooking," the woman said. The woman went into the kitchen and returned with a mug of coffee. She seemed self-conscious and almost shy.

Charlie Anderson came from the kitchen with eggs and a thick slice of fried ham. "Eat good," he said to the boy.

"He will," the woman said.

The boy wondered where the grief had gone and if his father had been so easily dismissed.

"We seen the end of a fine man," Charlie Anderson said and began to remove the dishes.

So the boy ate and watched them, these strangers. And then he walked through the house uneasily and went out through the kitchen door and stood beneath the heavily laden tree and shuffled in the snow and fingered the frozen bark while looking again to the far-off rim.

Eva came outside. The boy was conscious of her standing silently behind him. He blinked in the radiance and watched the high-flying birds, geese moving to feed and water. He heard the woman make a sound behind him, and he turned to see her face crumpling. She gasped slightly. She moved to him and pressed herself against him while she shook and wept. He stood with his arms at his sides and felt the softness of her breasts behind the sweater, and then nothing but the cold in her hair, which was loose and open against his face.

Then she was quiet.

"Let's go in," she said. "I'm cold."

She moved away and he followed her, oblivious to everything and completely drawn into himself.

"It will make you tough," his father had said.

"Goddamn you for this," the boy thought.

He slammed the door behind him and went to stand before the fire. The woman stood at the window with her hands behind her while Charlie Anderson busied himself with the dishes. The house seemed filled with the musk of the dead birds. The boy's numb fingers throbbed and ached as he held them open to the radiant warmth of the fire. "Goddamn everything," the boy said.

Clyman Teal: swaying and resting his back against the clean-grain hopper, holding the header wheel of the Caterpillar-drawn John Deere 36 combine, a twenty-nine-year-old brazed and wired-together machine moving along its path around the seven-hundred-acre and perfectly rectangular field of barley with seemingly infinite slowness, traveling no more than two miles in an hour, harvest dust rising from the separating fans within the machine and hanging around him as he silently contemplates the acreage being reduced swath by swath, a pale yellow rectangle peeling toward the last narrow and irregular cut and the finished center, his eyes flat and gray, squinted against the sun.

Robert Onnter, standing before the self-portrait of van Gogh, had finally remembered Clyman Teal, his expression beneath that limp sweat-and-grease-stained hat, the long round chin and creased, sun- and windburned cheeks and shaded eyes, a lump of tobacco wadded under his thin lower lip, sparse gray week-old whiskers, face of a man getting through not just the pain of his last illness and approaching death, but the glaring sameness of what he saw, at least trying to see through.

Changing position every few moments, as if from some not-yet-discovered perspective he would be able to see into an interior space he felt the picture must have, Robert Onnter faced the self-portrait of van Gogh

45

on temporary display in the marble-floored main lower corridor of the Chicago Art Institute and felt the eyes in the portrait as those of a man looking into whatever Clyman Teal must have seen while watching the harvest fields that occupied the sun-colored impenetrable August days of his life, the sheen brilliant and unresolved as light glaring off buffed aluminum: eye of van Gogh.

In the same place the afternoon before, people dressed for winter occasionally passing, Robert had been distracted by the woman, her gloved hand on his sleeve, while trying to visualize something he could not imagine, what lay beneath and yet over the texture of thick blue paint, how the ridged strokes fixed there changed his memories of slick wheatfield prints under glass in frames on his mother's wall. This morning he had left the woman sleeping in her cluttered brown apartment . . . her fragility only appearance . . . curled like a small aging moth on her side of a too-wide bed in a building that overlooked the northern end of Michigan Avenue and snow-covered ice of the lake, gone by taxi to his room in the Drake Hotel and showered and shaved and changed clothes, and feeling clean as when outdoors on a long-ago summer morning touched by dew that dampened the leather of his worn-toed childhood boots, caught another taxi and returned to stand again before the picture.

There was a sense in which he had come to Chicago to look for the first time at real paintings because of van Gogh. Part of his reaction against the insubstantiality of his life had been founded on those flat wheatfield prints his mother cherished. Robert smoked a cigarette from a crumpled pack, wondered if he should have left a note for the woman, and thought, as when the woman interrupted him the afternoon before, about his mother's life in isolation and her idea of beauty, surely implied by her love of those prints, desolate small loves in the eastern Oregon valley that was his home, the transparently streaked sheen of yellow gold over the ripening barleyfields under summer twilight, views of that and level windblown snow no doubt having something to do with the way he had felt compelled to spend this winter and with what he saw in the eyes of van Gogh, remembered from the simple death of Clyman Teal, and what he thought of his mother's idea, not so much of beauty but of the reasons things were beautiful. The woman's appearance beside him the day before seemed inevitably part of the education he had planned for this winter, escaping stillness. Except for two and a half years at the University of Oregon in liberal arts, studying nothing, a course urged on him by his mother, four years in the air force, a year and a half of marriage to a girl from Vacaville, California, named Dennie Wilson . . . when he lived in Sacramento selling outboard motors . . . he had always lived in the valley. So there was need to travel.

Twenty-seven when he returned to the valley, he worked for his father as he had always known eventually he would, spending his time at chores and drinking in the town of Nyall at the north end of the valley, seeing whichever girl he happened to meet in the taverns. Lately the calm of that existence had fragmented, partly because of his mother's insistence he was wasting his life, more surely because of constant motionlessness, reflected in the eyes of Clyman Teal and now in the detached and burning eyes of van Gogh. Robert had been disconnected from even his parents since the divorce, and now it seemed there had been no one even then. The girl Dennie, addicted to huge dark glasses with shining amber lenses, so briefly his wife, now lived in Bakersfield with another man and a daughter named Felicity who was nearly six

years old and ready for school. Robert could recall his
wife's face . . . the girl he married . . . could not imagine
her with a child, saw with absolute clarity the slender
girl from Vacaville, eyes faintly owl-like in the evening
because her suntan ended at the rim of her glasses. She
had grown up while he had not. By missing knowledge
of her strength in childbirth he had missed part of what
he could have been. His sense of lost contact was constructed at least in part of that.

The previous year, early spring, before winter broke
out of the valley, a morning he remembered perfectly,
he called Dennie before daylight, a frantic and stupid
mistake finally shattering any sort of relationship they
might have carried past divorce. Robert had been reading a book pushed on him by his mother, *The Magic
Mountain*, written by a German named Mann, which
seemed a strange name for a German, his mother saying
the book would tell him something about himself and
that if he would only begin reading he would see why
he must change. The day was a dead Sunday and he was
a little hung over and somehow bored with the idea of
another slow afternoon in the bars of Nyall, the blotched
snow and peeling frame buildings and the same people
as always, aimless Sunday drinkers. So he read because
there was nothing else to do and then for reasons he did
not understand became fascinated and began to struggle
seriously with comprehending what the German meant
by writing down his story of sickness and escape, seeing
why his mother might imagine it applied to him, yet sure
it meant something more.

He spent weeks at it, reading and rereading each page
and paragraph, savoring the way it was to be German
and writing about sickness, staying in his room and working at it each night, waking in the early morning before

daylight and thinking about it again. Until at four o'clock the morning of the phone call he turned on his light and began reading about a beautiful epileptic woman and began to feel as if he were himself at the next breath going to descend into a spasm and ended terrified and unable to focus his eyes on the print, or even move, as if the merest responses of his body might cause the heavy and shrouding weight of stillness to settle like a cloud blotting away all connection, and finally he forced himself and called the girl who had been his wife, Dennie, who he sensed might understand, might not have completely deserted him. She told him he was drunk and hung up quickly, and Robert felt himself alone in his cloud and could think of nothing but awakening his mother, begging her to make it go away, ended going for weeks through the motions of days surrounded by terror of something as simple as air.

Now the heavy and vivid symbolic color of the self-portrait seemed reality, the expression and agony of a man abruptly giving up, Clyman Teal who had been dying that last summer, a wandering harvest-following man who could have been van Gogh, who traveled north with the seasons along the West Coast in a succession of gray and rust-stained automobiles, always alone: hard streaked color of the painting ridged and unlike the wheatfield prints, actual as barley ripe before harvest, all bound into the stasis Robert was attempting to escape in this city, while traveling.

The woman's amber-colored hair was long and straight, over her shoulders, contrasting with the natural paleness of her clear oval face. She brushed her hair slowly. "I'd just finished washing it," she said, smiling, "when you called."

So casual she seemed younger, and small and full rather than tiny and drawn together by approaching age; she sat in a black velvet chair by a window overlooking the lake, lighted from behind by gray Midwestern sunlight, wearing a deep-and-soft-blue gown that concealed all but her white shoulders and neck, bare feet curled beneath her. Worn embroidered slippers lay on the pale, almost-white carpet in the room cluttered with sofas covered by blankets and with tables whose surfaces reflected intricate porcelain figures. "I like nice things," she'd said the night before. "Most of these things were my mother's. Is there anything wrong with that?" Robert told her he imagined not, and she smiled. "Call me Goldie," she'd said. "Everyone does." He had read the card inserted in the small brass frame beneath the entry buzzer. *Mrs. Daniel (Ruth Ann) Brown:* Her husband, she explained, was away in Europe. "He's no threat," she'd said. "He's gone for the winter."

They'd come here in the evening at her insistence, sat in flickering near darkness before the artificial fire, and she changed into a dressing gown and served tiny glasses of a thick pale drink that tasted like burnt straw. Finally he kissed her, moving awkwardly across the sofa while she waited with an ice-like smile. "He's away," she said, "to Greece, to the islands, to walk and think."

In the soft light of afternoon she was completely serene. Robert asked why her husband had gone. "Because of the clearness," she said. "The light . . . things have gone badly, with the unrest, and he wanted to think. . . ." Perhaps, Robert thought, he would follow, to the pale sunlight and dusty white islands and the water of the sea, New York and then London, Paris, Rome, at last to the islands off Greece, and see the water moving under the light, flow and continuity that might illuminate his vision of a desert stream low in a dry summer and water falling through crevices between boulders, always images of water, the cold Pacific gray beneath winter clouds, waves breaking in on barren sand and the heavy movement of the troopship just after leaving San Francisco for Guam, where he spent a year and a half of his air-force time.

In childhood he had imagined the barleyfields were water. After the last meal of the day, while dishes remained stacked in the sink to be washed later, they would all of them go out into the valley and look at the ripening crop, his mother and father, Robert, and his younger brother and even-younger sister all in the old dark green Chevrolet pickup. Now his brother had been dead eleven years, killed in an automobile crash his second semester of college, and his sister, married directly out of high school, lived distantly with children in Amarillo, Texas. Then they had all been home, and his father had driven them out over the dusty canal-bank roads until east of the fields, looking toward the last sunlight glaring over the low rim; and those yellowing fields were luminous and transformed into a magic and perfect cloth for them to walk on, and Robert imagined them all hand in hand, walking toward the sun.

His mother had named the largest field on one of those trips, and because of the prints in the house it had seemed she was only silly. But surely she had been right, however inadvertently. The yellowish, rough sheen of bearded, separate, and sunlit barley heads matched perfectly the reality of van Gogh, glowing paint, his eyes, texture. "The van Gogh field," she said, repeating it as if delighted. "It's so classic." They stayed until the air began to cool and settle and then went slowly home, Robert and his brother in the back of the pickup, watching the dust rise soft and gray as flour behind them and hang in the air, streaked and filmy as an unlighted aura even after the pickup was parked beneath the cottonwood trees behind the house.

Robert wondered what those evening trips had meant to his father. Nearly sixty, silently beguiled by sentiment, his father wept openly for a month after Robert's brother was killed, sat abruptly upright drinking the coffee Robert's mother brought, never going outside until spring irrigation forced him to work, after that revealing emotion only with his hands, gesturing abruptly and reaching to pick up a clod of dry and grainy peat, crumbling it to dust between callused fingers. During planting the man would sometimes walk out over the damp tilled ground and kneel, sink his hands and churn up the undersoil, crouch lower like a trailing animal. "Seeing if it's right," he would say. "If it's ready."

The woman returned with drinks. "I didn't think you'd be back," she said. "I hoped, but. . . ." She smiled, perhaps wishing she were alone, the last night an incident scarcely remembered. "I went back to the painting," Robert said.

"What are you really doing? I don't think I believe what you told me." She continued smiling. He had lied, unable to admit he had borrowed ten thousand dollars from his father, feeling childish over his search for places and cities missed, and told her he was an insurance salesman. "Looking for islands," he said, wondering if she would take him seriously.

She glanced away, stopped smiling. "The wheatfields," she said. "You should see them, the last particularly." Robert didn't answer. "Before he shot himself, I mean," she said. "When you think of what it meant to him . . . the yellow and that field pregnant, those birds . . . his idea of death, and remember it was there he killed himself, in that field, then you see."

"Yellow?"

"Simply love." The afternoon had settled, blue winter light darkening, her face isolated as if detached from her dark gown. "I don't think you can tell from prints," he said. "We had prints and there's nothing in them . . . my mother must have thought he was pretty and bright." Robert could not explain the insincerity of imitations, falsity.

"So?" The woman leaned forward just slightly, perhaps interested and no longer getting politely through an afternoon with a man she'd slept with and would have preferred never seeing again. Her tone was sharper, quick, and she sipped her drink, turned the glass in her hands.

"The way she acted. . . ." Robert stalled.

"Your mother acted improperly." The woman's voice was impatient, dropping the *improperly* as if she had changed her mind while speaking, finishing awkwardly, perhaps not wanting to acknowledge the moral distance implied in her judgment of him and his judgment of his mother.

". . . as if it were an example of something."

"Are you so sure? Perhaps it was all a disguise."

"I don't think she. . . ." Robert hesitated. "A man died and she knew some pictures and so it was beautiful and emblematic of something." His mother had stirred her coffee and smiled with total self-possession. "He finished doing what he loved," she had said. "Until the job was over."

The woman rose from her chair and began walking slowly before the windows, carrying a half-empty glass. "Women see more than you imagine," she said. "Sometimes, perhaps everything."

His mother: Duluth Onnter, what did she see, having come west from Minnesota to marry his father out of college, so taken by color and names? Her parents had moved from Minneapolis to Tucson the year after Robert was born, and although he had visited them as a child, he could not imagine the long-dead people he remembered, a heavy white-haired man and woman, as having lived anywhere not snow covered half the year. His grandfather had been in Duluth the day Robert's mother was born, and because of that had insisted she be named after a cold lakeport city. "Papa always said it was beautiful that morning," his mother told him. "That I was his beauty."

"Maybe the pictures were only warm and nice," Robert said. "Maybe she did see."

"My husband is like that," the woman answered, "imagines he's going to find spirituality in Greece, in some island. I don't. I'm lucky." She continued walking before the windows, gown trailing the carpet, her thin figure silhouetted. "I have what seems necessary and it's not freedom. I'll go Friday and confess having slept with you. That's freedom."

"To a priest?" It seemed totally wrong, sleeping with him and then carrying the news to church, the kind of circularity he had been escaping. "I don't see that at all," he said. "Why do anything in the first place . . . and pretend you didn't?"

"It's not pretending," she said. "It's being forgiven. I go to look as you do, somehow for a moment you helped me see better, look at van Gogh, and even my need to see is a sin, a failure of belief. I sold myself for what you helped me see. If that sounds silly maybe it is, but it wasn't to me then and it's not now. It's my own freedom and I don't need to go anywhere to find it. And it has to be confessed."

Robert wondered if she found him foolish, in Chicago, planning on Europe, if she wished to be rid of him and would regard his going coldly, as his mother had taken the death of Clyman Teal, if for her anything existed but hope. "I must seem stupid," he said.

"No . . . I just don't think there's anything like what you're looking for."

"Like what?"

"I don't know, but it isn't here . . . or Greece or anywhere."

"Perhaps I should stay." There was the easy possibility of a winter in Chicago, walking the streets, looking at pictures, going from van Gogh to Gauguin, Seurat, seeing her occasionally, as often as she would permit.

"I wouldn't," she said. "If I were you." Feeling denied some complex understanding she could give if only she would, Robert knew she was right and trying to be kind. "I wouldn't bother you," he said. "Only once in a while, just to talk."

"No," the woman said. "I'll get your coat." Her face was hard and set and he thought how melodramatic she was with her insistence on futility. Standing in the hallway with her door closed behind he saw how much she believed she was right, her belief founded on quick sliding glances at whatever it was van Gogh and Clyman Teal had regarded steadily in their fields of grain.

The next morning he returned to the Art Institute, and she was there, standing quietly in a beige wool suit with a camel's-hair coat thrown over her shoulders, a thin and stylish, nearly pretty woman who was aging. "You came back," he said. She turned as if surprised and then smiled. "Let's be quiet," she said. "The best part is silence, then we can talk."

Beside her, sensing she now wanted some word from him, Robert was drawn to the fierce and despairing painted face, memories of Clyman Teal in the days before he died. Summer had been humid, with storms in June and a week of soft rain in late July, and the crop the best in years, kernels filled without the slightest pinch and heavy by the time harvest started in August. Clyman Teal arrived the day it began, lean and thick shouldered, long arms seeming perpetually broken at the elbows, driving slowly across the field in the latest of his rusted second-hand automobiles, a gray two-door Pontiac. He rubbed his eyes and walked a little into the field with Robert and his father. Dew was just burning off. "Came last night from Arlington," he said. "Finished there yesterday." He'd been working in the summer wheat harvest just south of the Columbia River, two hundred and fifty miles north, for twenty years, always coming when it finished to run combine for Robert's father. After this job ended he'd go south to the rice harvest in the Sacramento Valley. Thick heads of barley drooped around them, and Clyman Teal cracked kernels between his teeth and chewed and swallowed, squinting toward the sun. "Going to be fine," he said, "ain't it, boy?" Leaving the trunk lid open on the Pontiac, heedless of dust sifting over his bedroll and tin-covered suitcase, he dragged out his tools and spent the rest of the morning working quietly and steadily while the rest of them waited, regreasing bearings Robert had greased the afternoon before, tightening chains and belts, running the machine and tightening again, finishing just as the noon meal was hauled to the field in pots with their lids fastened down by rubber bands. They all squatted in the shade to eat, then flipped the scraps from their plates to the seagulls, and the work began. With the combine motor running, Clyman Teal motioned for Robert to follow him and walked to where Robert's father stood cranking the old D7 Caterpillar, dust goggles already down over his eyes. "When there's time," he shouted, "I want this boy on the machine with me." Then he walked away, climbed the steel ladder to the platform where he stood while tending the header wheel, and waved for Robert's father to begin the first round.

So when there was time between loads, Robert rode the combine, learning to tend the header wheel, what amount of straw to take in so the machine would thrash properly and to set the concaves beneath the thrashing cylinder, adjust the speed of the cylinder according to the heaviness of the crop, regulate the fans that blew the chaff and dust from the heavier grain. "Whole thing works on gravity," the old man said. "Heavy falls and light floats away."

Sometimes the old man would walk behind the machine in the fogging dust of chaff, his hat beneath the straw dump, catching the straw and chaff, then dumping the hatful of waste on the steel deck and slowly spreading it with thick fingers, kneeling and blowing away the chaff, checking to see if kernels of the heavy grain were being carried over. "You need care," the old man said. "Otherwise you're dumping money."

But most often he just rode with his back braced against the clean-grain hopper. The harvest lasted twenty-seven days, the last swath cut late in the afternoon while Robert was hauling his final truckload on the asphalt road up the west side of the valley to the elevator in Nyall. Returning to the field in time to see the other truck pulling out, a surplus GI 6 × 6 converted to ranch truck wallowing

through the soft peaty soil in low gear, Robert waited at
the gate. The other driver stopped. "Claims he's sick,"
the man said, leaning from the truck window. "Climbed
down and curled up and claimed he was sick and said to
leave him alone." The combine was parked in the exact
center of the field, stopped after the last cut. Tin-eyed
and balding, the driver lived in the valley just south of
Nyall on a sour alkali-infested hundred and sixty acres
and now seemed impatient to get all this over and back
to his quietude. "Your daddy wants you to bring out the
pickup," he said.

Robert drove the new red three-quarter-ton International pickup, rough and heavy, out to the combine.
Clyman Teal lay curled on the ground in the shade of the
machine. Robert and his father loaded the old man into
the pickup, and Robert drove slowly homeward over the
rutted field while his father supported Clyman Teal with
an arm around his shoulders. The old man grunted with
pain, eyes closed tightly and arms folded over his belly.
Parked at last before the whitewashed bunkhouse, they
all sat quiet a moment, nothing in the oppressive empty
valley moving but one fly in dust on the slanting windshield. "We'll take him inside," Robert's father said, and
Robert was surprised how fragile and light the old man
was, small inside his coveralls, like a child, diminished
within the folds, his odor like that of a field fire, sharp
and acrid. They left him passive and rigid on the bunk
atop brown surplus GI blankets. He opened his eyes and
grunted something that meant for them to leave him
alone, then drew back into himself. The window shelf
above his bed was lined with boxes and pills, baking
soda and aspirin and home stomach remedies. Robert's
mother carried down soup and toast that evening, and
the old man lay immobile while Robert's father washed

the dust from his face. They tucked him under the blankets and the next morning the meal was untouched. That afternoon Robert's father called a doctor, the only one in Nyall, and after probing at the curled figure the doctor called an ambulance from the larger town fifty miles west. It was evening when the ambulance arrived, a heavy Chrysler staffed by volunteers, red light flickering at the twilight while Robert helped load the old man on a stretcher. Clyman Teal was sealed inside without ever opening his eyes, and Robert never saw him again. During the brief funeral-parlor ceremony six days later he didn't go up and look into the coffin, nor did anyone.

Operated on the night he was hauled away, Clyman died. "Eaten up," the doctor said, shaking his head: "Perforations all through his intestines." Robert remembered his mother's reddened hands gripping the tray she carried down the hill, his father's fumbling tenderness while washing the old man's face, the mostly silent actions. Three days after Clyman died the sheriff's office located a brother in Clovis, New Mexico, who said to go ahead and bury him. Six attended the funeral, Robert and his father and mother and the truck driver and his huge smiling wife and a drifter from one of the bars in Nyall. The brother was a grinning old man in a greenish black suit and showed up a week later. He silently loaded Clyman's possessions into the Pontiac and drove away, heading back to New Mexico. He hadn't seen Clyman, he said, in thirty-eight years, hadn't heard from him in all that time. "Just never got around to anything," he said. But the trip was worth his trouble, he said. He'd found hidden in the old man's tin suitcase a bankbook from Bakersfield showing total deposits of eight thousand some odd dollars. He said he thought he'd go home by way of Bakersfield.

The woman took Robert's arm. "I've had enough," she said. "Let's have a cup of coffee." Seated in the noisy cafeteria, she smiled. "I liked that," she said. "Standing there quietly together . . . that's what I first liked about you, that you knew how to be quiet." Robert wondered how often she did this, picked up some stray; what had driven away her husband. "Is that why?" he said, involved in a judgment of her that seemed finally unfair, perhaps because it came so close to being a judgment of himself.

"You could appreciate stillness . . . the moment I love in church is that of prayer, silence before the chant begins." Her hands moved slowly, touching her spoon, turning her cup, "I've changed my mind," she said. "I'd like you to stay the winter."

"You could go with me on Sundays," she said, "and see how the quiet and perfection . . . the loveliness on Easter."

But he couldn't. It was useless, for her perhaps all right, he couldn't know about that, but stillness while they chanted, and not her church or any city in Europe, even clarity of water, would do more for him than going home to those cold wet mornings in early spring while they planted, the motionless afternoons of boredom while the harvest circled. "Yes," he said, not wanting to hurt her, knowing he might even stay. "I could do that." Wheatfields reared toward the sky under circling birds, evening dust hung behind his father's pickup, and his brother's childish face was staring ahead toward lights flickering through the poplar trees marking their home, the light yellow color of love, van Gogh dead soon after, nearby.

When they were young they'd walk out on early spring-time mornings, into the vast greening and endless Kansas wheatfields his family had been accumulating through generations, since coming from Russia in the 1870s. They would burrow out of sight in one of the gullies, spread a blanket and oil up. "Let's just work at it," Jennie would say. Her face would glisten with sweat. She'd say it out loud. "Fucking." She'd grin.

Decades later, over martinis, Billy said he'd once thought Jennie hung the sun. "Once?" Jennie said. She found a sort of terrific Japanese restaurant in Kansas City, and they feasted on what she called purity, sashimi and Bombay martinis.

Even if that evening didn't cure the boredom, Jennie said, they shouldn't quit on romance. The next spring, as they were driving in southern France, the discovery of prehistoric painted caverns in the gorge of the Ardeche River was announced. Billy read about it in the English language *Herald Tribune* while they were eating breakfast on the square in Avignon. "Lions," Billy said. "They've never found paintings of lions before."

But no one would even tell them, when they went to the Ardeche, where the caves were located. So they went to see the nearby site of a famous atrocity, a stone village that had been abandoned after the Nazis had shot all the inhabitants, children included, when they were forced to withdraw from southern France. Wildflowers were blooming, blue and orange. Jennie wouldn't get out of their rented Peugeot.

Near Lascaux, the most famous of the painted caverns, no longer open to the public, Jennie consented to let Billy lead her out to an available cave, called Font de Gaume. "This," Billy said, "will be the actual thing."

They went in the early morning. The young French woman who led them to the cave wore a golden silk blouse, silver beads, and black and white Nike shoes like the grade-school kids wore in Kansas City. After weaving along a trail through knee-high grass across a flowering meadow, they came around a grove of trees to face a plywood doorway into a limestone cliff.

The stone cavern was like a trail, cool and narrow, undulating and absolutely dark except for a light carried by the woman leading them. Billy whispered that his hands were shaking. "Like going into an animal," Jennie said. Their leader shone her light on a line of buffalo painted on the bulging limestone above their heads, and reindeer with great sweeping antlers, creatures meandering toward the entrance as if they might escape into the sunlight and the good grazing down by the river.

The young French woman was holding her light in a way designed to illuminate curling etched lines connected to reddish strokes of ancient paint. "Reindeer," she said to Jennie, speaking English in her French way. "Kissing," Jennie said.

The doe, it had to be the doe because she didn't have antlers, was on her knees facing the interior of the cave. The male was bent to her, licking at her, both their tongues reaching to one another. The sweeps of paint were his antlers. All the rest was cut into the stone itself, etched in tiny incised lines. "They're kissing," Jennie said. She took Billy's hand.

God in heaven, Billy thought, this is pathetic. He began trying to think about lunch, some of that perfect soup, and goose liver pate. And, fuck it, he thought, this time a bottle of fifty-dollar wine. But by noontime he was asleep in a bedroom overlooking the river, and Jennie was on the side porch in the heat, face up, naked and sunning her entire body.

BE CAREFUL WHAT YOU WANT

Pinkie and me came from Montana to the highlands on Steens Mountain, nearby to where we used to live, to the old sheepherder's camping ground in the aspen grove at Whorehouse Meadows. Grace, my sister, traveling with a new boyfriend, was there ahead of us.

Eighty miles to the west, across the cold desert and into northern California, I could see the shadow of Bidwell Mountain. We ran close to 7,500 mother cows between here and there. Three generations of our people lived in that country where nothing flows to the sea and people take care of their own individual selves. Which is the way we lived until Pinkie and I decided to sell the ranch and take the money. We turned that country life into all the first-class airplane tickets you'd ever want.

Grace relocated in Santa Fe.

Travels like a racehorse was what they used to say about Grace, when she was running her roads. Lean and sun-dark herself, Grace was wearing a pair of wide-hipped white shorts, clean and ironed, but very short. There they were, chorus-girl legs on a woman turning forty-three, purple flecks from broken veins hardly noticeable. She had mud on her bare feet and was touching her tongue to her teeth.

"This one is Vito," Grace said, and I figured, Yeah, that one is Vito. He was leaning against a little buff-colored two-seater Mercedes—Grace always traveled in style.

Just one sober Sunday morning telephone call, and Grace had lured Pinkie and me into serious family medicine. Grace was in love again, and out of money.

So this lad with the rings on his fingers, and no shirt in sight, this was Vito. Maybe twenty-six, twenty-eight, too many rings, grinning and shy as a new dog while Grace did the talking, one of those suntanned boys who finds you when you got some dollars in your pocket.

Vito was half-owner of an adobe motel on the outskirts of Taos, called The Submarine, and Grace had moved her Indian art gallery into his building. As Pinkie said, that mean little streak she can show, "Paying to hook up her business."

"Vito, you come over here," Grace said. "These are your new relatives."

Our Woman, as my father liked to call my mother, named Grace out of hope. "So maybe she'd be different than your father and me," my mother would say, grinning.

My mother was one of those ranch women who go horseback after cattle while some hired lady keeps the house. Nowadays she lives on a mountain north of Santa Barbara, looking out over the Pacific, she's big in the Nature Conservancy, and she blesses me for selling the ranch. "Otherwise, after your father died," she says, fixing me with those blue British eyes, "I'd of never left that son-of-a-bitching desert."

The aspen were turning, leaves lime green and dead fading yellow in the late sun. In the morning there would be a rim of ice around the water bucket.

And here comes this Vito, barefoot and gimping over to meet us. "Pleased," Pinkie said. "I'm pleased." She moved out in front like she will at any echo of hostility from me. It's a sign of common sense. Good large-hearted Pinkie, gone thinner over the years, her red hair tight to her head, gone to wire and bone.

"You and me got private business," I said to Grace.

"Business," she said, "can wait. We better have a drink. Everybody is dusty."

Pinkie and I do our drinking as the sun is going down. Gin from half-gallon bottles with plastic pour-spouts. Pinkie has horses and I have my workshop, hard-handed things we do on our hundred-eighty acres of timothy meadow in Montana.

We got what we wanted. Not that we are entirely local. We fly out. We've lived a month beside the Dordogne River in France, and on the ridge in southern Spain, nearby to Ronda. We travel to London and Mexico, and eat the finest meals you can buy in Paris. Not having work means you invent yourself or take a chance on losing your nerve, drifting into craziness like you read about in newspapers. Some numbskull shooting his dogs and saying it was done on instructions from God.

In the early morning I brew coffee Pinkie buys direct from dealers on the Kona Coast, and I read. Sounds schoolyard, but I was the only man in our part of southeastern Oregon with more than one hundred books in his house. Books like *The Divine Comedy* with full-page pen-and-ink illustrations, along with a *Book of Common Prayer* so fragile with age I don't open it anymore. Now I have practical books, about shotguns and blacksmithing, field guides to the Himalayas.

When we visited in New Mexico, Grace showed me her bowls from the Mimbres Valley. The natives laid them over the faces of their dead with a hole in the bottom, so the dead could breathe, and decorated them with dancing birds going round to end up back at themselves. She said she'd found her own world. But Grace sold those bowls from the Mimbres Valley.

At sunup in Montana, at home in the Bitterroot Valley, I water banks of flowers around our log house, setting the stage for the fine warmth of afternoon and the honey-bees and hummingbirds. I hose down the stone patio and go to my shop, to the smell of steel and brass and hot oil, and turn on the lovely humming of the lathe. I create custom shotgun and rifle barrels and rebore old ones. There's a good market for such items, so I don't feel useless. The flooring in my shop is oiled, glowing under fingers of light in the late afternoon when Pinkie comes in from her horses and we have earned a drink of gin.

"One drink," Grace said, and she gave off that little breathy laugh. I cracked open the back of the Blazer, and got into my ice chest where the Tanqueray and lemons were cold and heavy. Pinkie dug our crystal glasses from the padded leather case, and I rattled the hard ice and poured that thick clean odor of gin from the bottle.

"You!" Grace said. She was looking at me. "Before anything, now, you shake hands with Vito. Maybe we will have a drink, then. Just maybe."

So I did it like a soldier, took his hand, which was dark and dry and hard enough to make you wonder what he did for work, and Grace just fluttered her fingers, taking her first sip of gin. Vito, he lifted his drink in that strong hand, and said in an accent from Europe, "Praise to every one thing."

"You and me, sister," I said to Grace, "we have to talk our business in private."

Grace lifted her hands like she was helpless and sad but going anyway. Nothing had changed in our way of negotiating distances. Vito smiled, all the bright teeth in the world.

"You kids." Pinkie said. She edged over to Vito and got her thin freckled arm around his naked waist. "Don't take it so hard," she said, hugging him. "You got me." I had to wonder if his flesh felt dry. She snapped her fine teeth together a couple of times, like a bright country flirt.

Pinkie has been my wife since my junior year of Animal Husbandry at Oregon State, and she has been faithful to me in whatever she counts, so far as I know, and I cherish her for it like you do the place where you want your ashes scattered. But I can't read her mind.

Then I was driving, casting a rooster tail of dust, both Grace and me balancing our glasses of gin and the hot wind in our faces. We weren't talking any business, and not going anywhere but home.

My hands were shaking when I parked and we stood looking out over that land we used to own. I was trying to light a cigarette, the world I should have cared about around me and as untouchable as dreams you can't recall. I lifted my glass but didn't have anything to say. Every one of us has places to go sightseeing in their own history. So there we were, eyeing the old dream.

My great-grandfather came to the country as a single-room schoolteacher, and my grandfather ran borrowed-money cows on the desert and gave the whole of his life to acquiring property, and my father shaped those meadowlands to perfection—he owned eight thousand acres of swampland hay and some six thousand drained and irrigated acres of peat-ground barley and oat farming. When we left, that valley was running like a creature whose bloodstream is water. There is nothing better than a bright morning with barley seedlings coming up yellow-green in drill-rows.

Grace went in the rock-walled store at Diamond while I sat studying my hands, hoping nobody saw me.

You don't sell out in that country and keep any friends. Grace came back carrying a case of Budweiser bottles, lugging that case like she knew how things worked in this part of the world. The last afternoon light touched her, and the lilac and cottonwood stayed luminous.

"See anybody?" I asked. "Anybody you know?" Grace nodded like sure. She knew somebody in every country-side store within a hundred miles.

She snapped the tops off two of those bottles. Beer frothed over her hands. Evening came down as we drifted at eighty and ninety miles an hour along gravel roads, flipping the bottles at road signs. I was thinking about country dances and the stunned ride home after sunrise.

On the northern edge of the valley a lava-rock escarpment lifts some thousand feet above the swamps. At the foot there is a channel called the Narrows, where runoff water from the Donner und Blitzen River escapes to evaporate in alkaline pothole lakes. The Narrows was sacred to the Paiute Indians. On smooth-sided boulders that must have rumbled down from cliffs in some shake of the earth, they painted stick-figure pictures of snakes and men, and suns that represented days of travel or good luck to their thinking. There were thousands of chipped arrow-points down in the tules along the big slough, at least on a dry fall, before the anthropology students got there.

My people never paid mind to such things. I valued them but then mostly gave the points away after I found them. Should have left them where they were. The flower beds where Pinkie and I lived were lined with stone bowls the native women used to grind their seeds. I don't want to know who's carted them off since we left.

There were days when I crouched out of sight in these tules at the Narrows. Rafts of greenhead ducks and Canada geese came to set their wings and drop to the slow water.

John C. Fremont told of celebrating Christmas of 1843 at the Narrows with his U.S. Army troop on their way to California through the wilderness, isolated from all they knew, jittery in the presence of so much pagan sign. They drank what brandy they had, ration after ration, and fired their howitzers, round after round into the snowfall of 1843. The redhead ducks and teal and Mallards and snow geese and Canada honkers lifting to flight and clamoring in heedless accumulations, the sighing of their wings, must have driven those immigrant enlisted men to sadness as they drank brandy from a tin cup passed hand to hand and wished they were drunk. Grace and I started this run up on the Steens like we had business to talk, but here we went, just drifting into the old life, another childhood sort of venture.

A greasy old man was camped at the Narrows in a home-built trailer, by himself in a lawn chair, home-brew wine there beside him, stoking at a pipe the way those fellows do when they want you to know they are not going to hurry for anybody, nobody to talk at but an Australian sheepdog worth three hundred bucks to anybody with sheep to herd. But hell no, this dog is a pet.

"They was here," the old man said. "You sure got some friends." He grinned and clamped white store-bought teeth down on that pipe. "Shooting rifles," he said. One boot had the sole built up high for a leg that was shorter than the other. "They was shooting tin plates like they was somebody."

"Yeah," I said, like this made sense.

"They sure as hell didn't kill any time waiting for you," he said, pointing his pipe toward a cheat-grass hill slope, glaring like he could see them yet.

"Piss-poor friends," he said.

"You should have a drink," Grace says. "You could use a drink." I should have got Grace back in the Blazer and given up ideas about John C. Fremont.

"You got any George Dickel?" the old man asked, and Grace laughed like she couldn't get enough of his surprising ways, and sipped at her beer.

With the headlights off I could see Steens Mountain dark against a sky coming full of stars. I searched for some sign of our fire up high among the aspen. But no. Must have been too far away.

"Shooting and drinking," the old man said. "Well," he said, "I got a bottle of Dickel. If that girl would help a man, and pull it out of the trailer in there, on the counter."

"Girl?" Grace says. "Kiss my ass." But we passed his bottle. "Them assholes," the old man said. "Shooting holes in anything."

Grace just shrieked. "Assholes! You are the asshole. We never heard of them people." She sounded gone in a way I had forgot and should have remembered. You get Grace drinking and you have got the consequences.

The old man squinted like he had never seen such a mouth on a woman. Grace showed a little slippage as she went to stammering, like some switch in her brain had flipped.

"I seen you plenty of times, darling," he said, talking to Grace like she was his specialty. "I worked over in the Caterpillar shop, on the ranch." His fingers were knotted with broken and mended bone, the nails black for life, some of them gone. He stank of sweat and diesel.

"No reason you should remember," he said, "but I know you. I seen you driving up and down the road, high fancy woman with the top down on a Buick in November, four or five trips a day, like you was on a serious business."

"No wonder," he said.

"No wonder what?" Grace had herself somewhat back together. I was thinking this old fart better watch out.

"No wonder you come out dressed like some Broadway woman. You ought to take a look at yourself. You people always thought you owned the country."

"We did," Grace says. "The whole damned thing." She was down close to his face, like she couldn't quit smelling him.

"In a whore's armpit." The old man was coming out of his chair, and I don't blame him much. Grace was ready to strike with that bottle of George Dickel. But I just twisted it out of her hand, feeling a sharp little snap from a bone in her wrist. For that hesitation I thought something was broken.

It is remarkable how anger can seep into you, and then you have cracked some man on the skull, or broke an arm, and you are standing there with no place to go. Truth is, you could kill somebody. One move like that and your life is gone. You have to keep track and catch yourself. So I confine my drinking to gin in the evening, with Pinkie. Or try to. It seems like a lesson you have to learn over every couple of years.

"You people were nothing but circus," the old man said, "all your lives." He was glaring, that little jumped-up son of a bitch, and I could feel the spray from his shouting. I dropped his bottle next to the white-eyed Australian sheepdog, and for another time I knew why I'd gone to Montana, where nobody had ever worked for our wages and never would, and could kiss my ass if I was rich or poor.

The old man dragged that heavy foot in the gravel, his face gone soft. "Augh, the hell," he said. "There's nothing so bad." Then I knew him.

The name just came to me, and I said it. "Whitney Bosworth." This man had worked for my father when they were young, and my father bought Caterpillar tractors to plow tule ground. I'd seen this man's name written into those payroll books in my father's schoolboy handwriting.

"Whitney," my father had said, "is one of them bunkhouse lawyers." This Whitney Bosworth was a man who thought he knew better than the man who writes the checks.

"God all hemlock," the old man said, and he was grinding his store-bought teeth. "Why the hell couldn't you keep anything straight?" He clenched his pipe hard in his mouth and took my hand in one of those callused hands of his.

Right away we were at each other, grip to grip, and he was as solid as cast metal. For all the steel I've hammered in my hobbies, he was stronger than me.

My people worked this country like they had a right. Truth is we never owned one thing worth counting. I could see it in the old man's eyes. He didn't want nothing of mine. Then his force went limp, and I stumbled forward. He jerked his hand away.

The old man showed those white manufactured teeth, dismissing us with a wave, turning his mouth down in a sour way as he hammered his pipe against the side of his thick-soled boot, knocking the fire on the ground. I climbed back into the Blazer, and watched him start packing tobacco into his pipe. Grace came in on the passenger side without persuasion. Thank God, because right then I would have drove off and left her.

No matter how hot the days, the high country in the Steens goes cold at night. It was full dark when we got back to the bridge across the Donner und Blitzen River. Grace had been sniffling, tears running down her face.

There were times when Grace drank for weeks in a row. She said there was nothing to get her out of bed on any specific morning. I knew what she meant. Even with property, I suffered disquiet, which edges at me yet. I am fifty-two years old, and I have managed to keep all the money anyone would ever need inside America, been married to somebody fine as Pinkie for a lifetime, and it is not enough, not for me, and not for Grace.

But you figure how it could have been helped with people like us, who got their way one time too often. Spoiled is what Pinkie says, being hard on Grace. And she is talking about me, I know it.

I couldn't listen to that sniffling and parked by the bridge across the Donner und Blitzen, the headlights showing out over the ripple of water.

"Grace," I said. "We got to sober up. It's a simple thing. We got to wash our faces."

"You'll drive away."

"Here's the keys," I said. "You got the keys. Nobody can drive away." I took her hand and gave her the keys to the Blazer. I had a spare ignition key stuck to a magnet under the hood. I have seen people toss a set of automobile keys far as they can, out into a creek, leaving everybody afoot.

We made our way to the water, me holding Grace so she didn't fall, and we crouched there splashing our faces with the cold water coming from snowfields. We were drying our hands on the tails of my shirt when Grace caught me with a sucker punch.

Grace is a ranch girl, and she has fought men in her time. It was a short punch, all her shoulder behind it, right into the solar plexus, and I went down to my knees.

Grace, she's the long-legged girl, all her life. "Damn you," she said, hard-eyed in the headlights. "What I'm going to do is marry him," she said. "Like it or not."

"Sure you are," I said. We held there, me on my knees, Grace not giving an inch, and then she reached me her hand.

Grace has been married to five men, one of them twice—a steelworker named Banjo Spaulding. She never talked about Banjo and claims she don't know where he's gone. Which was no tragedy, however she would play it.

"But Banjo was something," she'd say. "Nothing you could figure, but something." Maybe for her. Grace was working at the ranch, filling the summer as a substitute bookkeeper, a make-believe job while she dried out from another episode. After the Fourth of July, haying about to start, Grace started home from Burns with seven hundred dollars' worth of fresh produce for the hay-camp cookhouse. Six days later we found her station wagon hidden out back of the Deer Mount Tavern. The doors were locked and the windows rolled up tight, and that load of groceries was alive and multiplying in the July heat. Had to sell the station wagon. The man who bought it ripped out the upholstery but never did get rid of that dead-vegetable stink.

Grace called collect around the end of August, from Minot in the Dakotas, saying she had met up with Banjo in the Safeway and run off to marry him again. She wanted money to come home.

But that was lifetimes back. She pulled me close and

there we were, against one another on a creek bank in a desert night. She was shivering enough to shake the rings off her fingers.

"We should go swimming," she said, and I marched her back to the Blazer. After my first year of Agriculture School at Oregon State, where I was flunking Elements of Agronomy and Plant Pathology and didn't give a shit, I came home to sit in the moon shadows under willows along this creek after swimming naked with Grace. In the fall she'd be going back to a school in Arizona where she would learn the arts of marrying. Men inherit, in my people's way of proceeding, and women marry their luck.

"What they teach you," Grace said, "is fucking for money." She was just out of childhood, and we sat there on the grass, looking up the hill to the lights of our house, and I hated her, thinking somebody were already at her.

After that summer I went back to Oregon State and married Pinkie out of the Theta house, a big black-and-white-tie December ceremony inside the Presbyterian church, Pinkie glowing like porcelain in that white dress as she came toward me. We made our deal with the devil and got away clean, me and Pinkie.

And now in the headlights Grace was smiling like her heart would shatter, little tight lines coming together around her eyes like she knew all my secrets and could weep. "We'll be swimming in shit," I said, "if we don't look out."

Who would think I'd find myself transported by that pure lofting of sentiment that I have learned to recognize as Mozart clarinet concertos, and Bach on the flute? That Mercedes had speakers that could shatter crystal, and music was drifting through the aspen, so loud it seemed to flutter the yellowing leaves.

Sparks from the bonfire were flying, and Pinkie and Vito were dressed for the night, Pinkie in a bright orange ski sweater that belonged to Grace, and Vito in a tan flannel shirt from the Orvis catalogue. Grace laid her hand on my arm. "He's a good man," she said. "He does good."

"We opened the wine," Pinkie said, "to breathe."

This Vito had taken the rings with their heavy stones from his thin fingers before he started slicing on the flesh of melons, slipping those rings off one by one and lining them out like a row of decorations on the dashboard. His name was Vito Stasser, and he had lived the first seventeen years of life in Bombay as the son of a German Lutheran missionary before running away to the Netherlands and London and eventually New Mexico.

And he was some cook. The trunk of the Mercedes was packed tight like a Chinese box: four coolers, bottles of wine, and saucepans. I watched him handle the little pan in which he melted the butter over a bed of coals, and peel cloves of garlic. Those dry dark hands. You could imagine him butchering.

"Hippie," he said, looking up from a Dutch oven where he was stirring green chili without beans. We ate cheese warmed by the fire, a salad of melon and fruit in their juices, sour thick bread spread with melted butter and garlic and honey, and green chili dense with molasses and shredded veal and pork and marinated lamb and backstrap venison, all tasting of spices from God knows where in Mexico.

"See," Grace breathed. "See." There was no need to see. I was always going to give her the money anyway.

We sipped that first bottle of dark wine and loaded crackers with elk filet shredded and seasoned the night before, brought to us packed in dry ice. Not even Grace was drunk anymore, even though we kept on with the bottles of heavy red wine.

"One day we will all come to America," he said, lifting his gaze to mine with what looked to be innocence. He claimed to be German and yet his eyes were brown like a meadowland animal.

"My mother," he said, "she was related to Pakistani." I thought of the dark women who nowadays manage motel desks all over the West, and the smell of curry seeping out into the lobby like a yellow-flowered cloud.

"Anyways, we got the world," Grace says. "And if we don't, who cares?" Nobody, I guess. Try to figure why it's us who gets the bounty, people who make such a sadness of themselves while never letting go.

Undreamed shores and crystal cities. I think of my mother on her mountaintop overlooking the Pacific and wonder what it is, precisely, she labors to conserve. "Myself," is all she will say.

This Vito was showing off. So I was jealous like a schoolboy and wanted to demonstrate the degree to which our lives in this vicinity had been exceptional when I dug out my four-battery Police Special flashlight and headed out through tangled sweet clover into the trees.

Before World War I, thousands of sheep grazed those highlands, and the whores in Burns would load tents and cases of whiskey and take their work to the mountain. They put up tents, built fires in the night, and were hostesses at a great ongoing party. Herders carved the papery bark of the aspen with crossed bones, skulls and wine-glasses and whiskey bottles, and spread thighs, the split peach of vagina and buttocks between, wounds in white bark swelling out and distorted where the sap had run and healed. I sought to show the degree to which those women and herders had escaped ordinary commerce, that nights there on the mountain were a long way from the cribs where those women worked the winter out in Burns.

But as we stumbled through leaping shadows, Mozart ringing and Grace tracing her fingers over the incisions, lost and touching her tongue at her lips as if she could taste smoke and smell the sheep, I saw that no such escape from ordinary commerce is possible in any long-term sense.

Grace and I, we were traders, merchants. Stars were pinholes of light, Mozart rang, and Grace went on fingering cunts carved into the bark of aspen trees. I shattered my flashlight, a backhanded snap of the wrist, the aluminum tubing breaking, then darkness and my panting in the quiet. No one said anything.

Our fire was small in the distance, the shadows from the trees dappled over us in the soft illumination from the low moon, and I was back and lost where I'd been one late night in March in the days when I was still on the ranch, out under misting rain on a slippery levee bank, checking the water down by the 100-horsepower Dodson Lake pump, when the knots in my brain came untied. That 24-inch circular pump ran balanced so perfectly with its fine electrical whirring, and the purpose for everything got lost in the humming.

It was like losing your grip on a wrench, which falls in its slow startling way to vanish in the water below. In the electric humming, unable to fathom reasons for my hands in the dash lights, I was dizzy while soft rain pattered. There was no reason to stand there forever or not. Maybe such moments are secret to everybody, and not ever mentioned.

Sounds like foolishness, but it was not laughable. Far off, the lights of our house were flickering in the rain. Pinkie was there, and that was the secure thing. I nursed my pickup home over roads greasy with springtime mud.

Down in Santa Fe with enough money to last if she plays it right, Grace has turned her gallery into a school for artists from the pueblos who work with epoxy statuary of heroic dimensions. She calls every so often, maybe trying to sell me something like a red plastic buffalo, big as a Buick, edged in neon. We were raised to think we could walk on water, and then there was a time when it seemed like there was nothing actual, like maybe the world was a joke.

Lately, Grace says you have to be able to name what makes you crazy. "It's you," I tell her. "Grace, it's you." I wonder what she sees when she names craziness.

"Grace," I say, "it's the untouched thing that keeps you moving."

"Stay hungry," Grace says.

DO YOU HEAR YOUR MOTHER TALKING?

They offered me work in the mill when the woods closed down, but we had enough money and I hate the cold and ringing of the night shift, everything wet and the saws howling. So I stayed home with Ruth.

This is one of those company towns the logging industry builds on its second-growth hillsides. You can stand at our big window and not see anything but the dripping roofs of green frame houses below us in the brush and piles of split wood covered with plastic tarps and old swing sets and wrecked cars, most of them without glass or tires, which are bright and washed in the rain, and stained with rust, and you can watch the rain dimple the puddles slowing black and wet on the black asphalt, and you can wonder.

The place where Ruth parked her DeSoto was empty, and I figured she must have gone down to be at the Mercantile when it opened. My Chevy 4x4 was on blocks in the shed behind the house. I thought about spending the afternoon getting it ready to ship south again. I could feel myself leaving. It surprises me even now. It was a dream in which Ruth was staying behind forever. For a long moment I couldn't even get myself to see her face, or understand how I had come to this yellow-painted kitchen in Alaska. I blew my breath on the window and rubbed my initials in the steamy place.

The coffee was heavy and sweet, so I poured another

cup and lit up another cigarette. Some days nothing moves. You can look out at the evening and see the fog that was there in the morning, feathering off into the canyon where the river cuts toward the ocean.

What saved it was Ruth's old DeSoto. She had the headlights glowing. Ruth drives slow and careful.

Outside you could hear the water in the river. I stood on the porch, holding the coffee cup, and watched her park.

Ruth had a paper sack in her arms, and stepped around the puddles until she was beside me. Her hair was wet on her forehead and the shoulders of her cloth coat were soaked. She grinned and shoved the sack at me, and I knew I wasn't going anywhere.

During the winter Ruth can look blotched and strange. Some nights she will go alone to a movie and come back after I am sleeping. "Turn off the headlights," I said, and I took her sack.

Ruth ran back through the rain and stuck her head inside the car door and fumbled at the switch. Her skirt was pulled high and it stuck to the backs of her legs, and I could see the dark net of veins behind her knees.

In the summer, when we met, Ruth was deep brown from the sun and her legs looked like something out of pictures. She was working nights as a cocktail waitress in Brownie's and sleeping away her days on the beach. I caught her there early one morning and I woke her, not so much to start something with her as interested in why these runaway women act like they do. You see them in the mill, dirty and wet and working too hard and determined to be single as possible. And this one was a flirt at Brownie's, which was the other thing.

She told me she could always sleep if she was listening to the ocean, and she smiled and didn't look unhappy with me at all. Her hair was long and yellow and she was hard and tight enough, even after two kids, but she was a little too easy.

That was the first thing I'd heard about her. That she had two kids living with her first husband, but she was eager and not bad. She never talks about her other life and has never hinted at going to see those kids.

She slammed the car door and came back.

"I got bacon and eggs and juice," she said, taking the sack. "I'm going to cook a regular breakfast."

The fields smelled of fire. You could imagine little runs of fire burning behind the combines. My father would shred the heads of the ripe barley between his callused hands and blow away the chaff and bite down on the kernels, chewing like they were something to eat. I would lie on my back, hidden down in the barley, breathing in the smell of burning while the stalks rattled in the breezes.

All I could see was the sky. Ruth might have been with me, listening and quiet. That would have been a fine childhood thing, me and Ruth.

Ruth smiles when she looks away to the window where the rain runs in streaks. You have to wonder who she sees in her reflection, and what kind of family she sees in me and her.

We live on a big cedar-forest at the edge of the Japanese Current, where it never snows. Everything comes in by boat or floatplane. Ruth and I do not tell each other much of what we came from, letting it go at the fact that we are lucky, and here.

The first morning, after we woke up in her bed, she came along to spend the day with me. It was her funeral. Before noon we were down in the tavern, which is a

dark old barn built of cedar plaking and shakes, called
Brownie's since it was built in the early days of this town.
No one knows who it was named for. Big smoky win-
dows look out to the street, if you want to look.

All winter while it rains people gather to sit around
a barrel stove welded together from sections of culvert,
looking at the little isinglass window in the door, where
you can see in at the fire. The shadows run up the walls
and over our faces.

"We can give them something to talk about," Ruth
said that first morning. That's when I said it was her
funeral. I should have told her I was proud to walk in
with her.

That was October, and I was already done falling
timber for another winter. The low clouds hung down
into the fog coming off the seawater. That afternoon we
sat outside Brownie's under the veranda, on the wood
bench where everybody has carved their initials. We had
our cans of beer and we were out of the rain as we
watched the two nuns go along with their tiny steps on
the board sidewalk. You could see the trouble they had
taken to make themselves precious in the world.

"They think it's something," Ruth said.

I'll give myself some credit. Right then I knew this
wasn't just some woman from the night before.

The dark red bedsheets are part of Ruth, and her saving
graces. She changes them every day. She says winter is
underwater enough without damp sheets.

The rain was flushing through the galvanized gutter
above the window. Ruth would be in close beside the oil
stove and reading. I could see her, wrapped in one of the
Hudson Bay blankets I bought in Victoria. She keeps a
pile of magazines on the floor beside the new platform

rocker that was supposed to be mine after we moved in together.

Turned out I like to sit at the kitchen table, under the bare bulb. Ruth wanted to put a shade on the bulb, but I said no. There is a big window in the kitchen. I can see out into the canyon through the mirror of my face on the inside of the window and imagine the runs of salmon, and the old Tlingit fishermen in their round cedar hats.

My father and my mother were sleeping and I stood in the doorway and watched them sleep in the square of moonlight from the window. I walked away beside the shadows of the long row of poplar trees that ran between the irrigation ditch and the road from the house. Over on the highway at daybreak, while the sprinklers turned their arcs over the alfalfa, I hooked a ride on the back of a stake-bed truck. The last thing I saw was the trees along the high irrigation ditch; I can still see them clear as yesterday.

The cardboard patches Ruth nailed over the knotholes are already turning green. At least we didn't buy the house. I was right about buying the house. This is not the house we want. We want to build a house of cedar logs.

Ruth always keeps a big jug of orange juice in the re-frigerator. It burns away the taste of my cigarettes. That first night, in her cabin on the beach, Ruth said she had grown up learning to sleep naked. I can almost taste the feel of her.

All this winter my boots sat over by the wall, ready and oiled for the day when I can go back into the timber. You have to wonder what there is to like about falling those virgin-growth cedar trees, and what kind of man would stay with timber-falling long as I have. The cedars are the most beautiful trees in the world.

I go to the woods with my saw, and I work alone, which is dangerous, but I want silence when I shut down the saw. The red-grained back-wedge comes falling out, and I shut down my long-bladed Stihl, and I sit there letting the quiet settle in. The sawdust smells like some proper medicine. Right then I have enough of everything.

The first-growth trees fall true as angels, with the whoosh of their needles through the air, and they are dead. Like the natives I have learned to tell the trees I am sorry, but not so sorry I won't cut another in the afternoon. You kill to fill your belly, and then you tell them it was necessary.

You have to smile at such things.

It is my best life, out in the woods, and this winter there have been times I ache for it as I sit through the rainy afternoon in Brownie's and listen to the talk of fish. I wonder if falling trees is a true work. But I forget such worries as Ruth and I walk down through the dripping early darkness to the movie house, and we are saying hello to everybody and Ruth is excited like a girl.

"I walked in the rain," Ruth said. "After you went to sleep I walked in the rain."

"You got to tell me what was wrong with you," she said, and she ran her cool fingers down the long scar on my inner arm.

Each step of it seemed right at the time. I can see the pale tender skin along the inner arm separating as the blade traced toward the wrist, my flesh parting along the length of my wound in a perfect clean way, and the tough white sheath and the deeper seeping meat before it is all drowned in blood.

I am telling you about craziness. I lay in those beds

and I thought I heard my mother's voice and never slept until I came to believe there was some tiny thing wired into my arm, and electrical circuits flashing along with their messages, right at the core of my arm like a little machine, and all of it a trick. Then I could sleep, because I knew someone could cut it out with a surgeon's blade.

The idea got me in trouble. I found out about doctors, and I went into the office of the best doctor in Klamath Falls. I asked him to cut the wiring out of my arm, and the crazy part was cutting on myself when he refused.

It seemed like a good idea to think my troubles could be solved by the touch of what they call micro-sharpened knives. It was the kind of thing you come to believe like babies believe the things they learn before they are born. It was like knowing which way is up. But the trouble with me is over. I sit in our kitchen and read hunting magazines, and I imagine stalking waterbirds like they were my friends.

I am telling you about craziness, but I wouldn't tell Ruth. "We all been born with too much time on our hands." That is what I said.

We have nights to think about our earliest memories. In mine there is a red dog resting in the dust beside a stunted little lawn juniper and the crumbling concrete walkway.

There is a thunderstorm breaking.

That was out front of the apartment building where we lived when I was a little child in the farmhand town of Malin, on the northern fringes of the potato land that drops toward Tule Lake and California. My mother walked me on the sidewalks, in and out of the stores, and to the barbershop where they smiled when I climbed up to the board across the arms of the chair.

That red dog barked in the night, but usually he was sleeping and wrinkled in the dust. What I see are heavy drops of rain. I can still count them as they puff into the dust. I can close my eyes and call up those raindrops striking each by each.

Like my mother would say, "Each thing in its place." I can hear her voice clear as my own.

My father had his two hundred acres of barley-farming property out south of the Klamath Falls airfield; he was hiring winos to herd his few hundred head of turkeys, and he always had my mother. I would ride out with him in the gray pickup truck, gone to check on the well-being of his turkeys, and then home to my mother.

Him and my mother, in those good years after the war, they called themselves the free world. But they were playing it like a joke, at parties, with other men and women.

Men would come to the kitchen while my father was gone, and my mother would pour whiskey. They would sit at the kitchen table with their whiskey in a tumbler, and my mother would laugh and stand beside them, and those men would hug her around the waist and smile at me while they did it.

"You better go outside," my mother would tell me, and she would already be untying her apron.

"We was late with our lives," my father told me. "Me and your mother, so we just stayed with our playground." He told me there was too much room for running with your mind when he was growing up in Tule Lake during the Great Depression. He said he went crazy during those years, and that I should be careful if I got my imagination from him.

My father told me this when I was thirteen, maybe as

a way to explain his lifetime. That was the first time I left, wishing I could hear my mother say good-bye.

"If you won't answer me," Ruth said, "I was only going to tell you what happened." She was at the stove, tending the eggs and bacon.

"You were feeling bad," I said, "and you had a few beers and you walked in the rain and felt better. Like nobody ever did."

"I drove down to the ocean," Ruth said, "and walked the beach. Before daylight." Her back was to me. She was turning the eggs. "It was nothing but that and I felt better."

Ruth colors her hair golden and it was running with seawater when she came walking up from the summer ocean. Ruth shook her head, and I knew her face would taste of salt. Right there was the first time she reminded me of my mother. My mother was young, and her bare arms were red in the summer rain. The drops stood in her dark hair as she was laughing in the yellow light under the thunder.

It was just before the Fourth of July and hot and clear and still when I came north. The low fog was banked far out over the ocean. After some drinking I would see the gray summer tide coming cold over the sand and think about the Lombardy poplar trees you could see for twenty miles over the fields of alfalfa on the right sunny day around Tule Lake. If you imagined them clear enough those trees would come closer until their leaves were real, like they could be touched.

Crazy is really a place you could learn to stay. You could learn to live there forever. It was a reason for drinking. I never imagined myself into somewhere else when I was drinking; it was only afterwards.

Down in Victoria I bought myself a whole set of Alaska clothes as if that would turn me into an Alaska man, got me a barbershop shave, and rode the Alaska ferry north. It wasn't the right way to travel into such a place, but it was easy at hand and it was the season for seeing seabirds and all the fishes from whales on down.

The days were warm and sunlit and you could smell the evergreen trees over the diesel exhaust as we came to dock in midafternoon. I walked out over the sandy flats to the ocean, a wind was coming off the fog on the horizon, and I found a stone fireplace where fish had been cooked. The sand was littered with red berry boxes, and there were torn newspapers in the brush. You had to wonder who had been there.

By nightfall I was sitting on the bench outside Brownie's, listening to some men talk about the salmon run and lumbering. The inside of Brownie's looked hammered out as a cave. I thought of the mills where I have worked, the howl of saws and wet sawdust, and I wondered if I had come to another wrong place as I sat there being a stranger in the side-angle lights outside Brownie's.

Give it a summer, I thought. There was nobody to notify. I had my clothes folded into a canvas warbag and a half dozen thousand-dollar bills. My chain saw pays me a hundred and fifty dollars on a good day. Only a fool does things without money.

"We ought to be married," Ruth said. She was washing the few dishes and stacking them in the open-faced shelves above the sink. She went on placing the dishes carefully atop one another, then dried her hands and went to stand before the oil stove. "I could have another baby," she said. "It's not too late. That could be my calling." She smiled like that was going to be funny.

I got up and walked away from her and went into the bedroom. After closing the door, I sat on the bed. *That could be my calling.* I couldn't hear a thing from the other room, not even Ruth moving around. After a while I pulled my worn old black suitcase from under the bed. With the suitcase open the next move was easy. Ruth could come and stand in the doorway and watch while I packed.

"I'll take a little money to travel on," I would say.

She would look down a moment, and her face would show no sign of anything, and I would think it was going to be easy to get out of here with no trouble. "Watch me," I would say. "I'm gone."

When the suitcase was packed I would head past her into the other room, pull on my slicker and leather cap and go out to the shed where my Chevy 4x4 was up on blocks. It would be dry inside, with the rainwater splattering from the cedar eaves. The dirt is like dust mixed with pine needles.

There is a pint of whiskey hidden under the seat in the Chevy. Two long swallows and I would think about laughing and sit in the dirt with my back against the wall and whistle *ring-dang-do, now what is that.*

My mother beat my ass for that song, and washed my mouth in the irrigation ditch. It's a song I think about when I want to remember my mother and the way she laughed and hugged me as we sat on the grass with water coming from her hair in little streams. Now that is not crazy, thoughts of the water streaming through the little redwood weir in that irrigation ditch and my mother knowing some joke I didn't understand.

Ruth came and sat beside me and my black suitcase

on the bed, her elbows on her knees and her head down and her hair hanging forward like she was a wrecked woman with nothing to do but study her hands while some man made up his mind about her life. "My mother told me a joke about times like this," I said.

Ruth didn't answer.

"My mother told me everything you got is like a China cup," I said. "Because it never came from China, and you always got to worry if it's going to break."

"Some joke," Ruth said, and her face was an old woman's face when she looked up at me.

Not that Ruth was crying. Her eyes had just gone old, and the strength in her flesh had lost some of its hold on her bones. Her lower lip fell down, and her teeth were stained by so many cigarettes. I could see the years to come, both of us old in some house where she looked like my mother and the radio was always playing in the other room.

Long ago, before Alaska, out at the Klamath Falls hospital, a nurse unlocked the door and I walked into my mother's care, a man thirty-four years old and unable to even trust his own brain.

My mother's hands were cold. What could I tell her? That I had lived too long watching my father turn hermit in the house he built on the corner of his property out by the airfield where the air-force pilots flew jet planes every hour or so like a clock. Could I tell her jet airplanes will make you crazy for answers to everything?

She showed me an old photograph of my father: a young man with just the tip of his tongue between his white teeth, and his hands deep in his pockets and the brim of his city-man hat snapped down over one eye, like the picture-taking was going to stop everything for all time at this moment in his schoolyard. Behind him you can see the painted sign: *Turkeys.* "He was the best man they ever had," my mother said. "Now he's made you crazy."

You could take the same picture of me, deep in my forest beside some fallen cedar tree, and you might think, *Who the hell does he think he is?* We've all seen pictures of men who are dead now, with their long saws crossed in front of some great stumpage, and their sleeves rolled up over their elbows.

My mother puckered her soft mouth as she eyed me and didn't talk anymore, as if her tongue had locked and she had lost her speech. Then she shook her head. "I'll tell you the joke," she said. "This is the joke of it." She looked around at the house where she was making her stand; expensive hardwood furniture and a mantel decorated with half a hundred engraved stock-show trophies. Silver spires with imitation silver Angus bulls on the top.

She didn't look like anything was a joke.

"Things changed," she said. "Things will change." She was trying to make it sound like a hopeful notion. I imagine the first lie, and a time when they came to know there was nobody to trust. I imagine them coming to want every goddamned thing they could get their hands on. It's simple. You are going to die, so you'd better get in on the money and the screwing.

One afternoon she took off in a Lincoln Continental with a heavy-built man nicknamed Cutty. "Cutty had this house left over from the time he was married," she said. "Your father wouldn't even take me to bed. Cutty knew better, right from the start."

She took off those frameless eyeglasses, and cleaned

them. There was a box of Kleenex on every table in that house. I picked up one of those trophies with the little silver Angus bull on top, and I thought like a child, so this is the way to be rich.

The fall-of-the-year sunlight percolated into my mother's house through layers of gauzy curtains, and she never went outside. Twice a week there was a cleaning lady, and every day there was a boy delivering things. My mother just cooked me meals and waited for me to make my peace.

There was nothing to know. Maybe it is true about my mother and Cutty. Maybe they are a great love. Over the years Cutty has worked himself up from auctioneer to purebred-cattle breeder. He was always sending flowers from Bakersfield or some show town. She said it was his busy season.

For nine years I worked my summers in the woods and batched through the winters with my father in his house. On winter afternoons I would drive over to the Suburban Tavern and shoot some pool and come home to stir up some tuna and noodles for the microwave oven. Nobody, my father or me, ever really cleaned up the kitchen, and more and more I started to feel tuned to the trembling of those microwaves, all the time closer to discovering I had been wired for other people's ideas.

Just a quarter mile south of my father's house there's a barroom built from a Quonset hut back in World War II, with gas pumps out front. My father is still eager for a walk down to the bar and some drinking and talk first thing in the morning. It's just that you can learn to live in some of those stories. But that is enough about craziness. It's a place you swim like deep in the black ocean with strange fishes. You might never want to come up. It's a country where I could go visit and find a home.

Ruth refolded each thing I owned, her hands trembling as she filled that black suitcase. The unshaded overhead light was on bright in our bedroom, and she moved like an underwater creature. "Fine," Ruth said. "Just god-damned fine."

Her face was flushed with that fallen look you might imagine as secret to animals, her eyes glazed like stones and this way and that quick as lizards. I remember my mother late in the night when she was drunk in our kitchen where the windows were glazed with ice. I would come awake from hearing her laugh and ease from my bedroom where the people's coats were piled on the other bed, and she wouldn't even see me with those eyes.

"Just fucking wonderful," Ruth said.

"You pitiful son of a bitch," Ruth said, and I didn't know if she meant me or her.

Ruth unfolded my stiff canvas Carhartt timber-falling pants with the red suspenders, the cuffs jagged off and the knees slick with pitch, and she stepped into them and pulled them up and hooked the suspenders over her shoulders, her dress wadded up inside, and she stood there like a circus girl. "How do you think?" she said. "You think I could work in the woods?"

"You ought to have a baby," she said. "You ought to lie down on your back and come split apart and smell your own blood in the room."

"But you never can," she said. "What can you do?"

This is what I could do. I could lace my boots, and I could get the blocks out from under my Chevy and spend the afternoon cleaning the plugs until she idles like your perfect sewing machine. It would be twilight and the white Alaskan ferry boat would be rolling in the long ocean troughs as I stood at the rail with a pint of whiskey in my hand and watched the cedar-tree mountains turn to night under the snowy mountains beyond to the east. I could go anywhere in America. But Ruth was smiling, and it wasn't her sweetheart smile. "You better get me," she said, and she dropped those suspenders and stepped out of my canvas Carhartt pants.

"You know what I can do?" she said. "I am going to lie down and come unseamed for a baby."

You wonder what the difference is between men and women, and if women really like to think there is some hidden thing inside them that is growing and will one day be someone else, some hidden thing telling them what to do. There was Ruth at thirty-nine years old, with her babies behind her in another end of the world, too old for what she said she wanted, standing there with her hands open and willing to look at the possibility of dying for some baby.

You think of the old explorers. You have to know there was a time when they smelled their land from out to sea and the clouds blew away, and it came to them that this coastline they had found was a seashore where nobody exactly like them was ever given a chance to walk before.

"I'm going to say, baby," Ruth said, "do you hear your mother talking? Baby, are you listening?"

Me and Ruth were there in the glare off the glass; I could see us, and I had to wonder what our children would see if they were watching and looking for hints about who they should come to be. Ruth looked mottled white like the blood was gone out of her. "Either that," she said, "or you can get the hell out of here."

Those old explorers must have studied their mountains, trying to think this was what they had always wanted, this place they didn't know about. You try to control the shaking of your hands, and you want to say, all right, this will be all right, this is what I'll take, I'll stay here.

"We'll split some shakes," I said. Teetering around that room, picking up my stuff and storing it back into where it belonged, refolding those stiff Carhartt pants along the seams, carefully as they could be folded, I felt like a child on a slippery floor and Ruth eyed my moves like all of a sudden she wasn't sure what she wanted after all. Ruth could see I wasn't going anywhere, and the rest was up to her. There was no one thing to say, and I still cannot name the good fortune I saw except as things to do.

"You coming with me?" I said. In this country they roof their houses with shakes split from pure cedar. We went out that afternoon and bought a straight-grain cedar-tree log, and had it hauled to us. Ruth wouldn't hardly look at me or say anything, but she went along.

That night Ruth slept in her chair with her magazines. By late in the next day we had built a canopy of clear plastic to keep our work dry from the rain, and we started splitting the shakes, side by side. We will build a house where our things to do can be thick with time on our hands.

People will watch us build, and we will be the ones who know the secret. We'll watch strangers on the sand flats. We'll know they envy us our house built of cedar logs. We will live with one garden that grows nothing but red and yellow flowers, and we'll have another garden with cabbages. Our dogs and our cats will sleep on the beds, and me and Ruth will carve faces into the cedar-log walls. Those faces will smile back at us in our dreams and be our friends, looking back at us like we were the world, and watching what we do like we watch the seabirds picking on the rocks at low tide.

There will be cabins with covered walkways to the house. My father could live in one, and my mother could come visit, and Ruth and I and my father and my mother could all go down to the movie house and over to Brownie's after the show.

Your mind is full of little animals and you have to trick them with things to see. We will live in our house like the old people lived in their houses. Maybe we will come to know what it is like to lie awake in the night while our children listen for our talking and laughing as we listen for theirs.

Sharon understands the uses of beautiful. When she comes to visit, even in this middle life, she wears her hair down and schoolgirl-thick to her shoulders.

I think of her walking the streets of Seattle in her high heels, carrying a little black umbrella and going to lunch with the rich women, like you suppose they do, while men watch. I wonder if she piles her hair up and shows the back of her neck.

"Don't get too many ideas," she says, and that's a way of joking. It wasn't me that got us started.

Once I was the hired boy, and her mother sent me to drive Sharon through the open snowfields to the schoolhouse over on Two Dot Creek with the sun coming onto the peaks of the Crazy Mountains. Sharon was nothing but a cold bare-legged little girl, but I sat warm in her mother's Chrysler and watched her red hair bloom with the sunlight that bright winter morning. She looked back and saw me looking, and she still brushes her hair at night like a schoolgirl.

Which makes me happy to think about.

"Too bad Turkey couldn't come," Sharon said. "He loves it out here." That was bullshit. Turkey didn't love it at all. Sharon was talking about her husband, a Chinese man named Tony Lee, called Turkey by his friends, who are everywhere once you get beyond Montana. Turkey is a tall fellow with immaculate eyeglasses, a tough-headed guy who specializes in friends, and a chess master who flies out of Seattle to play month-long matches in Taiwan and Egypt.

Sharon and I were on the lawn in front of the house where she lived when she was the girl I watched. I keep that creaking frame country house painted white now that it is mine to live in. The sun was only up a half hour, and the bunkhouse hands were gone to the Fourth of July in Billings. Out beyond the corrals a thousand yellow butterflies were flickering through the wheatgrass.

Sharon sipped her Bloody Mary from my marmalade jar. The only glasses I keep these days are marmalade and peanut-butter jars. I eat off paper plates when I don't eat down at the bunkhouse. On the built-in breakfront in the dining room I keep a stack of paper plates about three feet high.

"Poor old Turkey," Sharon said, and that was more bullshit. There is nothing to pity about Turkey. You had to know he was a hard nut the first time I met him, the spring Sharon was a junior at the University in Missoula. They'd driven off to Reno in his Studebaker and got themselves married, and it was a scandal in our part of the world.

"Couldn't you get a white man?" her father said, which was mainly a way for him to break his own heart on Sharon, no matter how strong his feelings. Sharon and Turkey had just come east of the mountains for family introductions, over the Rock Mountains, as Lewis and Clark called then, and east through White Sulfur Springs to the low pass where you see the Great Plains make their endless start, and down along the Musselshell.

In those days I hung my coat and my hat alongside my snaffle-bit bridle and woolly shotgun chaps and spare shirts on a line of nails driven into the wall of a room in that bunkhouse the old drovers built of cottonwood logs when they first brought cattle north from Texas, and I slept there on a steel-framed cot, right at the heart of things where in summertime I could prop open the windows and smell the corrals after thunder and rain, and go to sleep listening to the horses as they clomped back and forth through the creek water like they will, on their way to some nighttime foraging or another. There are summer nights when the bunkhouse is empty and I still go down there to sleep.

Even in those days I was considered family enough and welcome in the kitchen door anytime I wanted, day or night. It was the afternoon before New Year's and the Christmas-tree lights were still plugged in and blinking beside the fireplace Sharon's grandfather had built of river stones. Sharon stood her ground, and Turkey just sat there without flinching and smiled through those eyeglasses, and you could see he was every bit as tough as Bert Doran.

"Shit," Sharon said, and she grinned. "The Chinese invented gunpowder." If that was supposed to be a joke, it didn't work. You had to know Bert Doran. He never smiled at all.

"Not that boy," he said.

Right there Sharon called for Turkey to come with her, and they drove off in his gray-colored Studebaker, and Sharon never came back while Bert was alive. Bert Doran was an oil-field roughneck come north out of Wyoming and reformed into marriage, and it was his luck to work himself to death just about the time he joined the Masonic shrine down in Billings and discovered the life he'd been expecting to enjoy. Sharon's mother owned the property and that was a lot of Bert's problem. For a while after she died and Sharon got the deeds I had the same kind of problem, but now we have found a floor under things.

Tony Lee is an engineer for Boeing in Seattle, and Sharon lives with him in one of those big old restored three-generation houses out on the cliff above the Puget Sound in Ballard, when he isn't off somewhere playing his chess. Which is where he was that morning, I guess, somewhere. I have spent my life seeing after Sharon's acreage in Montana.

"You can't trust them," Sharon said, and she swirled her drink with her forefinger and sucked it dry. The meadows out below us were greened up with swamp grass and the willow was in fresh leaf along the sloughs. My feelings for such mornings have cost me real money. Without them I'd be living somewhere else, on my own property. I like to live at an edge of the world where I know the stories are about people who lived there just before me and haven't been dead very long. Lewis and Clark named the Musselshell, and even they are not so long ago.

"Foreigners," Sharon said, and you had to know she was talking about Turkey. One time right after she inherited the deeds from her mother, when she was drunk and telling stories on Turkey, Sharon proposed calling this place, "The Japan Ranch." I made real sure none of the neighbors heard about that one. It was a name they would have laughed about and liked. If it had stuck I couldn't have lived here anymore. Nobody wants to live in the middle of a joke.

Sharon sat her drink glass down on the lawn grass, carefully so as not to spill, and she lit a Lucky Strike, same as Bert had smoked. This was a sign. I don't think she smokes any cigarettes in Seattle.

"Turkey is whoring on me," she said. "He has for years."

"He loves to drink in Trader Vic's," she said. "Isn't that a kick in the ass?" I kept my silence.

"Did you whore on her?" Sharon said. She was talking about the woman who was my wife the second year I was home from the air force on Guam. Becky, we all called her Beck, who has been gone to California this long time now. Sharon was looking at me with the gray steady gaze of someone solving problems, a city woman in her button-up Levi's and the old flannel shirt she had raided out of my closet. Now she was talking about whoring around.

"Yeah," I said. "I suppose."

"Good morning," she said. She walked out to the old poplar trees at the edge of the lawn, moving carefully, and picked at the bark with her fingernails.

"You know," she said. "I never liked her."

"She wanted to stay," I said. It was a lie. "Not really," Sharon said. "Not ever, really."

"How would you know?" It was a decent question. Sharon had only seen Beck twice in the flesh. "It's the sort of thing you know. I could have stayed. But she could never stand it. Right from the first summer I knew she was history." Sharon held her drink to the sun like she was toasting somebody. "But for me this could have been home, easy as not."

"You're out of drink," I said.

"You remember shooting quail?" she said, and of course I did. We shot quail from the greasewood in the horse pasture, fluttering hundreds of them rising from the brush, and I remember killing maybe a dozen with #7 shot as I fired Bert's fine-etched Belgian 12-gauge into the thick coveys on the ground. Her mother skinned them quickly, never bothering to pluck the feathers from such tiny frail creatures. Her mother cooked only the breasts in pale thick gravy.

"She could never stand it," Sharon said. She was still talking about Beck. "She stood it," I said, thinking of mornings upstream on the creek, where it comes out of the Crazy Mountains, and Beck bare-legged in the cold water, unhooking the small trout I caught while the mist burned off. Beck is my dark-eyed lost girl, who would have been my wife all these years. "She wanted to stay," I said, and it was the same lie.

"Another drink would be nice," Sharon said. "Then I'll cook your breakfast. I'll be your girl."

We had steak and eggs on my paper plates, and we ate on the oak dining-room table that was her mother's, the only substantial furniture left from the old days. Sharon's mother had polished that table with care I never understood until lately. I haven't bought much other furniture. Chairs, a microwave oven, a queen-sized bed, and in the living room I've got a pool table I bought from Ernie Brier after he went broke in his Harlowtown tavern. Sometimes I shoot pool and drink beer all night long. I shoot a decent game of eight ball.

"I guess I was jealous," Sharon said. "This is the place I should have lived. She had my house."

"I always wanted, years ago," she said, "for you to get in my bed when you thought I was sleeping."

"Sometimes yet," she said, "when Turkey's out at night, I lie in bed and think about it. I thought about it just now when we were out on the lawn. I thought I could live here and it would be all right."

"Yeah," I said, and I mixed us some more of the vodka and tomato juice.

"You know what I did?" she said. "I whored. One time I whored."

"Never mind who," she said. "We went to Trader Vic's and we went upstairs and screwed. We did it in a hotel room. Up in the elevator from Trader Vic's. One time I whored and listen to this." Her gray eyes were not steady anymore.

"There was a fire," she said, "we're on the nineteenth floor, and there's a fire." She chewed a last piece of steak. "I could hear sirens," she said, "and I'm bare-assed naked. Down below there's a fire, and you know it made me happy. I mean like when I was a little girl and there was something I always wanted to happen and it was happening, like a game and I was in a movie watching, little red trucks and hoses and people running around in the street."

"It was a hotel," she said, "down a hill a couple of blocks from our hotel. The Hotel Winslow. I don't forget it. Twenty-six dead people in the paper that morning." She told her story, like she had all the words learned by heart. "I looked at the pictures a long time. There was a fireman climbing a steel ladder. The windows above him were seeping smoke, like spirits getting away. That's what I think. Does that sound stupid? The curtains were afire. There was a list of names. I remember one for the sake of remembering. It's Jacob Crashaw, aged sixty-three, from Deloria, Missouri. Who the hell could that be? Somebody named Jake, he lives sixty-three years, come all the way from Missouri to some down-and-out hotel in Seattle so he can burn up in my movie.

"It was like it wasn't my real life," she said. "Flames were going up hundreds of feet, and then my fellow comes up back of me in my room, puts his arms around me and holds one of my breasts in each hand, and rubs his cock against the back of my legs, and I hated him. Come over here, he said. He pulled the drapes and I hated the son of a bitch.

"I tried to break the window," she said. "I tried to

break the hotel window with an ashtray. Can you imagine me jumping? Nineteen floors?" And I could, I could imagine her falling.

"I could have jumped," Sharon said. "If that glass would have broke. I thought about it later, and I knew right then I could have jumped." Sharon and I were knocking balls around on the pool table, and into the second bottle of vodka.

"I stayed the rest of the night with him," she said. "I was afraid of the elevator. I was sick, and he helped my head, and I felt like my eyes were crossed."

"Do something for me," she said, and she began unbuttoning her Levi's. Her underpants were pink under the tails of my flannel shirt. "Sit down," she said, and she patted the edge of the pool table. Then she kicked off her sandles, and shucked out of her pants, leaving them wadded there on the floor.

"Just sit down," she said. Her legs were soft white, and thicker than I had imagined. She took my hand and her fingers were cold as she folded mine to the cool flesh at the inside of her thigh. "Just hold me," she said. "Just there. That's all I ever wanted." My fingers felt like sticks.

"There's nothing wrong with this," she said. "I figured that out." She began unbuttoning the shirt and she was naked underneath as she dropped if off. I had not understood that her breasts were so small.

She took the lobe of my ear between her fingers and she leaned back away from me and pinched, and I sat quiet with my eyes watering, looking away from her to the scuffed hardwood floor her mother had kept so polished, and wondering if this was a contest. "Just move and I'll stop," she said. I closed my eyes and she let go.

"It's too bad this is what happened," she said, and when I opened my eyes there were tears running down her face, her eyes wet with her strangeness, and no one could have seen what she thought or wanted.

She lifted my hand from her thigh and stood from the pool table. My hand was damp when I clenched my fist. "You and the Chinaman," she said.

"Not me," I said.

"Close enough," she said.

"Nineteen floors," she said. "I could have fallen like a bird." I saw her falling, the glass shattering and Sharon pitching herself out into the air.

"Come here," she said. I touched her breasts as gently as I could, but they were cold. I traced my fingers to her nipples and she caught her breath like an actress.

"Hold me," she said. But I just dropped my hands to my sides. Sharon touched her cheek, like her mother would do. "All right," she said. "Now act right." She began unbuttoning my shirt.

In my bedroom the patterns of light from the windows were yellow and still on the dusty hardwood floor as I lay beside her in the noontime warmth across my old flannel sheets. Her body was glowing white as she sucked at my nipples like she had found something, her arms around me, pulling me up to her mouth. Then she gave it up and rolled back to look me over. "It doesn't mean a thing to you," she said, "does it?"

But then she smiled. "Jesus," she said, "but we're alone in here."

"I wanted to do something wrong," Sharon said, "and you're it." She lay back and lifted her arms and closed her eyes and seemed to be waiting.

At least she was warm now, those breasts tight as a child's when I kissed them. Once in a while there are times just before sleep when the darkness behind my eyelids comes bright with sky and waterbirds in their flyways, going north. Back of the house when we were children Sharon and I would sleep in the groves of wild plum with their heavy fruit, and the blue flies and yellow jackets would burn the air with their sounds. I could hear that burning in my ears.

Sharon took hold of me and I was ready as a creature can always be ready. But right there came the moment when I would not do it. I listened to the small birds rustle in the lilac outside, and closed my eyes and saw bright dust floating in the sunlight behind them.

"All right," Sharon said, and her voice was thick and caught, and I opened my eyes and since then I am not sorry for anything. She caught me looking as she rested there ready for me with her hands thrown back above her head, studying me and biting the tip of her tongue and looking close to laughing. I leaned forward and stared down into her dry gray eyes where nothing was happy and pinned her wrists as she raised those heavy white legs up around me. But it wouldn't work and I had to reach down and start myself into her perfect slipperiness and she sucked long breaths through her teeth.

She hadn't been fucking anybody much, for a long time, you could tell, because she was tight and too eager. For a thought I worried if this was a way women could do themselves damage.

"Goddamn," Sharon said when we lay back, and her eyes were glowing with whatever she thought, and she was still strange to me as I came back to myself. "I think about you," she said. "You never owned anything, and I got all this."

You find what fits, and you make your deals. That's what Bert Doran used to say. But you got to want it, Bert would say, like a dog wants his bone, and if you do, who cares how they work you?

The fields are blooming with wild lilies, and I'm not going anywhere. But there was something I had to know. I have never in my life owned a quarter inch of earth, and I was still capable of believing I didn't live anywhere if I didn't own the place I lived. That feeling took a long time to shake. Last February I went on a drive for myself, south out of this snow country.

In Las Vegas I ran a hard-way six into eight hundred dollars of profit and I kept driving beyond Hoover Dam like a rich man. I subscribe to *National Geographic Magazine* and I wanted to see some things. I looked at the Grand Canyon and the Hopi Indians and it was like postcards, and then some Indians.

But finally I got out of the pickup and worked my way down into the redrock canyon where they have preserved a prehistoric place called The White House. I waded the shallow twist of a wide creek three times to get there. Everybody this side of civilization has seen the pictures, the cluster of native mud brick jammed up in there onto a shelf under that great cliff. Those old people picked to live in a place that could only be reached by long ladders, and there hadn't been any ladders for centuries. The huge slick-faced rise of water-stained red and orange rock above it was as much alive as the soft little wind blowing down through the willow and Russian olive where I stood on muddy ground at the bottom. The moaning of the air sounded like get out of here, this isn't yours. There is nothing to own but what you do. We think it comes down to money and deeds to the property, but nothing ever does, except for fools.

On summer mornings I would catch my pinto horse— he was half Shetland and half Morgan and as quick a little horse as I ever owned—and I would gallop down the gravel roads and out into the chill air across the meadows toward the hay camp in the Cameron field where the hay-stacking crew was living in their tents alongside the round willow corral.

The cook fire would be lifting smoke and a few early risers would be sloshing their faces in water from the ar-tesian well and edging in toward the coffee. In mist that rose from the meadows as the sun cleared the Sagehen Ridge I would circle after our great Belgian work teams, fifty or so lumbering beauties, their hooves thumping the dry sod as I herded them along, and then I would climb down off my little horse and act like I was a grown man in front of Bert Doran.

Say what you will about Bert, he died of an over-worked heart in his middle age. When the teams were harnessed and snuffling at their oats we would breakfast on pounded round steak and gray milk gravy over bis-cuits, all of us at a table on the meadow grass outside the cook-shack door with Bert Doran at the head.

These days I sit at the head of that table, and that's what I own. "This was a good chance," Sharon said. For what I don't know. I still cannot read her eyes, when Turkey goes off and she makes her way out here from that big house in Ballard. She tells me her purple and white lilacs bloom in February and March, while our ground is still buried under snow this side of the moun-tains, and I think of going there, walking up the sidewalk and shaking hands with Turkey like my visit was some kind of good idea. But that would be a mistake. Sharon has got hers and I got mine.

Last fall before the serious snow we rode the frozen fields in my Ford three-quarter ton, and she asked me what I want to do with her property. I showed her fences and cattle-guards and she asked me if I didn't have any more ambitions than I was showing her. "Not a one," I told her, which wasn't all of the truth.

This spring I took her with me when I harnessed the Belgians to the stoneboat sled and sledded manure from the corrals across the swampy meadows, the rumps of those Belgians steaming in the sunlight and the trace chains clanking. I was out to rebuild the long dams that spread the water across the swales. This is where the notion of balancing water comes into the equation between us.

It's our way of describing the work, by which I mean leading water out from the redwood head boxes in the creek through high ditches, turning the water out from sodded ditches to spread in long even sheets against those low manure dams I build across the native grass-lands. In the winter I feed loose hay to the cattle with my same team of Belgians harnessed to the creaking hayrack sled and the long expanses of crusted blue wind-driven snow are like more water until you wander off into the drifts.

"Balancing shit," Sharon said.

The movement of water on her property is my finest example of how things should try to be. But don't imagine that I am dumb enough to think love is like water, except in the way everything is like water, always seeking to fill its level. I didn't say a thing and went on with grunting at my work as I forked that load of manure off the sled, and Sharon kept herself quiet until we were going home. "When I was a kid," she said, "Bert would take me along."

"Bert," she said. "Bert was a son of a bitch."

"You're going to die out here," she said. "Just like Bert."

"Fair enough," I said.

Bert whipped us all when it comes to example. Don't die before you've taken a try at enjoying whatever it is you always wanted, that's what Bert would tell you, if he was speaking to you from his gravestone over in the Harlowtown cemetery. And this is my ambition.

"Sure as hell you're right," I said. "Just don't bury me over there in Harlowtown, like they did to Bert." Sharon never answered but just smiled like a real snake and bit at the tip of her tongue like it was something too sweet to taste.

"Not on my property," she said, and it was my turn to keep quiet. "I'm going to sell it," she said. "I'm going to put the money into Kmart stores. What the hell are you going to do then?"

"Same thing I'm doing. For somebody else." It wasn't anything I'd thought about, but it was true. I only discovered it was true as it came out of my mouth.

"I guess," I said, and I told her one sure thing you can learn from only a little history of Montana east of the divide. "Nobody around here is in it for the profit."

"You figure there's any profit for living in Ballard?" she said, and she wasn't smiling anymore. "How about Ballard?"

It took me that long to figure out her talk of selling the property was only a way of jerking my chain for what she saw as my own good. Sharon just kept staring away over the fifty-mile swale of the Musselshell drainage toward the Big Belt Mountains, like she was waiting for me to digest an answer to her question, and she didn't say another thing until we were back in the house and I was pouring cold water into my automatic coffee machine.

"So you and me," she said, "you figure we got a family, where nobody else belongs." She had me there.

"Yeah," I said. "You and me."

"Since where?" she said, and she held out her right hand like she was memorizing the look of the lines in her palm.

"Not so long," I said, and she never mentioned another thing about selling the property. These are the lessons of adversity. I've burned my ladders, and I cherish Sharon beyond any dream of rich women in my bedroom. She knows I will feed her cattle and keep her fences tight, for whatever fences and money are worth.

We make our own little airplanes, and I fly mine. I will never own even the place I stand on the ground. When she comes, Sharon looks beautiful as she can manage for my eye. I repolish the dining-room table her mother had polished, and I fit precisely into my skin, a man who is happy as he needs to be.

. . . after Alicia's chastity I cannot describe the warmth.

Wild meadowgrass is mowed short inside the circle of stone wall, around the trash barrels and picnic tables. Broken glass glitters under the dry sun. A Nevada State Historical Marker decorates the entrance, a brass plaque mounted in a chipped concrete block.

> Late in June of 1892, the wagon party led by Jerome Bedderly, 137 persons, was without provocation wiped out while attempting to defend themselves within this corral. One Shoshone woman, a volunteer and guide, was also killed. Her infant child survived according to later stories. Indications of violence are clearly distinguishable on various stones. This was the "Sleeping Child Massacre." *God Rest You Pioneers.*

Jerome Bedderly stood on the sand hill to the east, among the sage clumps and bitter greasewood in the still warmth of June, contemplating his oncoming death, which he could anticipate so clearly. In his journal, which turned up in Virginia City almost a year later, finally making its way into the Bancroft Historical Collection at the University of California, Bedderly tells of standing transfixed while the people in his party walked in circles until a woman screamed, drawing his gaze to "the miserable children, lodged and staring eyes" while his hands trembled.

The frantic woman was his wife. "She signaled again from her madness our collective doom. Again I suffer fear and melancholia while knowing I must die, as in childhood I dreaded the futility of my prayer. My sin is doubt. Her voice was mine."

Paiute Creek runs below and to the west, named for Indians whose greater name was Shoshone, in a shallow valley of meadows and willow-lined sloughs, with rolling sage country beyond at the horizon. On clear days in June the DeFoe Mountains to the northwest stand unreal and close in noontime light, snow-covered and dim against the pale sky, revealing dark and steep canyons gathering watercourses to form Paiute Creek. Bedderly writes of attempting to calm his panic by concentrating on three ponderosas in a triangular grouping just at the snow line. The grove is still there, oriental and impervious to history, silhouetted faintly against the white in late June.

Her voice was mine.

Alicia Bedderly had been shrieking occasionally for more than a week. As for reasons, we know only what Bedderly wrote. "Her madness causes the grievance, not the tribesman's innocence." Alicia had been touched on the arm by one of the Paiute men. "Those dark inquisitive fingers, the white flesh of her arm . . . she never claimed she was harmed."

He tells of the first shooting. "The terrible landscape erodes out our goodness, bleakness violating our souls this last week of unforgiving misfortune. We wrestled our fear and aimed always westward with our remaining resolve and energy, and it began so gently. We were pleased to see the natives in this wilderness, anything human preferable to the unending desolation, greeted

them in a wholesome and friendly way though they were
the most uncouth we have seen, scarcely more than animals in their habits, with almost no charm, at the same
moment clever and redeemable, like childish circus rope
dancers, until Alicia's terror. The native attempted hiding in the brush but our young men dragged him to the
rear of my wagon. Alicia would not be solaced, accepted
no ministration, not mine nor a woman's, and her eyes
rolled and she frothed blood, having severely bitten her
tongue and the insides of her cheeks, and she fell down
and was mad, the affliction of women. To aid in her cure
I shot the native. Not lethally, in the thigh only, a fleshly
wound and warning to him and others, with hope that
appreciation of her security within my power might bring
Alicia to restoration. In turn his eyes rolled and he fell
faint. *The native pleaded and was doglike but in my resolve I
shot.* May God forgive me the possibility of error. . . . But
Alicia was not restored and I console myself with the
notion that she perhaps never truly believed, has always
sinned in secret fear."

"*. . . but it was my right to do so.*" As a boy in Kansas,
Bedderly witnessed the murder of his father by proslavery
vigilantes during the six-year underground war known as
"Bleeding Kansas." The late spring of 1857 his father was
found to be harboring an escaped Mississippi slave and
was shot down in the afternoon by seven hooded men,
falling to bleed on the baked ground near his own doorway, where the turkeys scratched. "Onward from that
day," Bedderly wrote, "I was unable to think, considered
mad and kept from school and other children. Of that
time I remember nothing. So I have always been alone."
He recovered during the Kansas drought and famine of
1860, twelve years old at the time, by suffering a midnight vision. "I found myself beneath the moon and again

aware of myself, unable to sleep, and I was relieved of my suffering by the justice of God while lying on the cool hard earth and feeling warmth from the depths to which my father's blood had soaked. I was human, and learned that goodness must be willing to injure as my father had been killed, risk deaths and force its own survival if needs be. From that moment I was restored and a model pupil, God's Hand."

Bedderly graduated from a ministerial college in Topeka and by the late 1880s had established a following of nearly three hundred hardworking "Hands of God" around the small western Kansas community of Divine Law, a town site chosen by Bedderly and now vanished under cornfields, abandoned when his vision of purpose drove him west seeking new land, opportunity to work in the Lord's Way. "We will cultivate immaculate fields and gardens," he wrote. "Our seaward progress is divine. The shade beneath our trees will be perfect and cool on the Sabbath. We will force perfection."

But his first contact was with natives who had almost certainly been forced, a group of "southwestern tribesmen" mingling with Shoshone of the Great Basin, who were a grandly poor, nomadic people who traveled the desert in small bands, always en route to gather food, possessing only the crudest portable tools, living in temporary shelters constructed of brush and terribly afraid of white men. It is hard to understand the gathering of nearly three hundred described by Bedderly unless they were together for some special and fated occasion that in turn kept them from fleeing before the squeaking and ship-like wagons, perhaps a final despairing vestige of the ghost dance, a revivalistic movement born at Walker Lake in western Nevada from the vision of a man named Jack Wilson, later known as the messiah Wovoka.

"The natives were encamped for a quarter mile around a small pool of greenish water, fresh though evil appearing, on the edge of a vastly arid and absolutely featureless alkaline expanse which reached beyond sight to the south and west. We were passing around the northern edge of that desert, seeking the water they occupied, when we discovered their makeshift shelters of brush. Mr. Slater was in favor of driving them off into the wastelands, knowing they could survive like animals, but I intervened, thinking we were all human and could exist together. We camped at the water's edge, displacing only a few of their huts, and they came seeking trinkets, and the rest ensued."

The leaders of the violence with which the natives answered the shooting were the so-called southwestern tribesmen. "More than thirty, Mr. Slater reports, are camped among the others, traveling west toward some pagan figure of prominence in their religion." One would like to think of these outsiders as some escaping remnant of the Comanche nation, greatest horsemen of the Americas running from the Oklahoma Territory where they had been surviving on dole meat. But it is more likely Mr. Slater was mistaken and they were not from the southwest at all. James R. Mooney, traveling in the west at the time while doing research for the Bureau of American Ethnology, reports that Sitting Bull and other Arapaho visited Jack Wilson at Walker Lake in the fall of 1892. Perhaps there is some connection. At any rate they were proud and carried good rifles, mostly Winchester Model 1873s, rode horses and reacted to Bedderly's shooting of the Shoshone man with a night of mournful singing and dancing. At daybreak they attacked the wagons, which had moved on during the night. The guide, Mr. Slater from Salt Lake City, was killed along with twelve other men. Bedderly was left alone in command, without knowledge of the country ahead, only the certainty that he must continue. "Bad luck is the excuse we give," he wrote.

After the fourth night of travel they were attacked again at daybreak, this time leaving their wagons to defend themselves above a rimrock. "My error, my fatal mistake," Bedderly writes, "but I thought only of sailing west before the driving wind of our vision with all my people." None were killed but the wagons were burned, stock slaughtered. "Our possessions are gone, our condition impossible without prayer. We continue on foot. Alicia is the same." They were waterless, followed by the straggling band of Shoshone, scouted by the distant and implacable horsemen. "We rest, help one another, walk while prayer burns the mouth. This desert is endless."

The woman and her child appeared the morning of the sixth day. According to Bedderly it was as if she simply materialized perhaps a thousand yards off in low brush, a small dark figure holding her swaddled child, seemingly unafraid as they approached. After gesturing she led and they followed. There seemed nothing else to do. That night they camped by a wide and swift-running stream that must have been Paiute Creek where it curls through the desert upstream and east of the meadows. "We gorged on water, burned willows, shot a deer, cooked. Men vomited during prayer and prayer ended. We are the creatures this desert makes us." They proceeded west in the morning, following the woman, arriving at noon on the hilltop from which they could see the whole of Paiute Creek Meadows. "The watery place which should seem a glorious refuge is now only a barrier to be waded, vile and boggy, desolate." There was no thin line of smoke lifting toward the sky, no sign of habitation or any sort of help, just isolation and the stone corral below, at the edge of the meadow.

Imagine five men and a string of packhorses in the cold early spring of 1890, mustangers, rain sleeting at them as they make camp near the creek. At the mouth of a stony dry wash they build the corral, prying rocks from lava outcroppings along the shallow rims, rolling boulders onto stoneboat sleds dragged by teams of mules with improvised harnesses, men sweating and lifting rocks into place, the corral slowly taking its circular shape. In late July it is finished and the men chop willows and build long wings outward from the single gate, the opening that faces up into the wash, waiting for wild horses, men running them in relays for nearly a week, always closer to the corral, the animals exhausted as they trot slowly down the dusty wash, crude willow fences forcing them onto the single path that leads through the gateway, into the corral. The stone wall is higher than a man's head, thicker than the body of a wrecked automobile. It is late afternoon, the horsemen are in the gate, facing the sun, the west, brims of their hats pulled low. For this moment they have saved whiskey. They drink, one rubs the back of his hand across his mouth, smearing white alkali dust in his month-old growth of beard. The herd stand listlessly within the rock walls.

"The builders are unimaginable," Bedderly writes, "Divine Providence."

The woman led again and there was nothing to do but follow, so they went down from the sandy hill and entered the corral, which seemed a refuge, sign they would survive, a found fort. "Now it seems a trap we cannot escape," Bedderly wrote three days later. "The natives wait."

Our seaward progress is divine. Who can imagine the true beginning . . .

Perhaps it was believing the myth of California, heading directly across the desert to the coastal valley where they intended settling near the present-day flower-growing center of Lompoc, traveling by wagon in an age of railroad, so they could bring along huge cherrywood tables and crated blue willow china, forgetting that Kansas is as close as anywhere to the still center of belief. *"Who can imagine the true beginning?"* Surely it lay somewhere east of the turkey-packed earth where his father died.

"They are going to attack," he wrote. "We are terribly hungry. Some are eating cooked grass. We do have water. Since sunrise I have known. God's vengeance." Then he tells of the night and that sunrise. "By gestures the Indian woman attempted curing Alicia. The screaming became constant and I held Alicia and after weeping she slept. The dark woman left her child and came to rest with us in the untrod grass near the wall and after Alicia's chastity I cannot describe the warmth. When I awoke the women were gone. It was not yet daybreak and birds were calling in the blue light. Alicia and that dark woman were naked in the mouth of the corral, Alicia's body pale as the morning and seeming to quiver even as she stood without motion. A huge and filthy mass of natives clustered perhaps a hundred yards beyond, silent while Alicia and that carnal woman faced them with hands joined. The native woman at last spoke in a loud voice, in her primitive language, reached to lift her child from the grass, naked and white. The natives turned muttering away and left. I thought we were saved, approached and saw the child simply fair against her dark mother, with blue eyes and wilted reddish hair. Alicia screamed again. Something I did not understand had been refused."

I console myself with the notion that she perhaps never truly believed, has always sinned in secret fear.

The people within the corral waited as the Indians retreated and grouped silently in seeming conference, a diverse scattering of figures on the gray and brushy hillside above the corral. "My sin and carnality did cause this and I would die if I could with grace and honor. Alicia refuses clothing, tears it off when the women attempt dressing her. The day is warm and perfect and we are hopeless."

So Alicia Bedderly's nakedness, her offering, brought nothing in exchange but death. "Thy will is mine," read Bedderly's final journal entry. "I have refused prayer and learned the warmth was only carnality." The attack began later that morning and lasted until movement stopped, gestures hanging forever in silent motionlessness, expressions to be studied while the scream waits to proceed. A stone to examine. Lichen grows in the crevices. The shade is cool; clear water flows through an imagined countryside near Lompoc; the scream dies away.

The vernal equinox of his eightieth year, calendar beginning of the spring he had been anticipating for no other
reason than warmth . . . an end to his constant chores
of wood splitting and fire building even though cloud-
less days could not be expected on that high desert
country of southeastern Oregon for another month or
maybe two . . . Jules Russel woke to immobility, mute-
ness, blindness. He was awake without even the ability
to see the outlines of his only window glimmering in the
darkness, alone in the single room of his cabin beneath
the bare and leafless limbs of cottonwoods planted by
unknown homesteaders just upstream from the break
where Horn Creek fed through the shallow lava rim
into the swampy meadows of the Black Flat. Listening
to the hesitant rasping of his breath beneath the more
insistent sound of spring wind moaning in the rusted
pipe of his stove, which meant the fire had gone out
and was no longer drawing, he imagined the shimmer-
ing desert to the west defined by shadows of summer
clouds. Attempting to move, to turn off the hip that
was paining him and must have awakened him, off the
wadding of his stained and dirty gray blankets, he found
the expected thing was at last happening; and although
he had been for months preoccupied with the idea of
death, anticipating it without regret, he now felt nothing
but the cringing animal within himself, and yet he could

127

not truly believe he was dying. Everything was the same, and he was imprisoned to await cessation like a living rodent within the darkness of a snake's digesting length, already engrossed in useless panic and wanting back his freedom to be always too old and cold and alone. He had desired death but this entombment was only that, his mind as it had been, granted nothing, no illumination or sight of shadowy pastures in which white-robed figures wandered, willows in the distance, no solace, only death. He wondered if this day was cold and overslung with gray and blank clouds, if the motionless sky to the east was occasionally inhabited by the quiet passage of ducks moving north, if it was daylight, morning. He had been imagining daylight without any way of knowing, just as he had imagined night without any way of knowing, the clock ticking on the table, on oilcloth whose pattern, so often traced when there was nothing else to do—faded orange roses with flecked green leaves that were perfect in his mind—the clock giving no indication of time, only ticking away its passage. It could be morning.

This isolation was more vivid and absolute than anything he had experienced in even the line camps, unpainted single rooms almost identical to this, near the springs on the desert to the south and west where he had spent so many of the later summers of his life with only the company of his horses and the mice. Terror came on him quickly and soundlessly as the motion of remembered dreams from childhood, while nothing changed. The sound of wind yielded to that of the swift clock and his mind spun on the center of pain in his hip.

Then as if falling through a barrier he became increasingly calm and began to think about being missed and discovered before death. Perhaps at the post office in Frenchglen when the check came. But that wouldn't be until he was dead and rotting and they would hate him more than they did. Maybe they would miss him anyway. Jules hoped for discovery so this isolation, while unbreakable, could be eased, so he could be moved off his hip and saved from dying in pain. So he could think clearly. There had to be another chance.

But that was hopeless. There was no one to come. People ignored him as he despised them. The men on the Black Flat were subjugated to their trucks and their grease and the cheapness of easy work, devoting their lives to pleasures he could not imagine, always the easiness. At least he had his disgust and willingness to be old and close to dying and ready to escape the sight of horses beaten by men forcing them into hollow aluminum trailers, everything smudged by the black grease from machines, impatient and rough men who lacked the nobility of their animals . . . and again as he had these winter months Jules remembered one of them, young, with a scarred face, his head strangely misshapen, who complained of aching dizziness before leaving a desert branding crew in the middle of a summer workday, whose saddled horse had come home trailing broken bridle reins, with its head cocked sideways. The young man's body had been found the next day, with open white eyes fixed on the sun, trousers down, dead of a stroke while defecating among clumps of tall sage along a dry gravel-strewn streambed. Jules had secretly found pleasure in thinking of that death, but now he envied the sudden closure of light and knew the rest of it meant nothing, all deaths being death, and wondered if that man had died in discomfort or relief from pain and wondered what he would do himself when his bowels filled

from the meal of stew and sourdough bread he had eaten
the night before. And if his own eyes were open, staring
sightlessly, fixed. He had no way of finding out.

But at least his mind was his own again, even though
his finest discovery at this extremity seemed to be that
death, when confronted as fulfilled expectation, could
not stay long before the mind of an aged man accus-
tomed to habitual concern with the minute functions
of his body. His right hip ached, the wind blew, the
clock untwisted its spring, the cabin creaked, something
rattled. His right ear, beneath him on the pillow, itched.
He wondered if death came like that, as an itch abruptly
erased, and he concentrated on the broken man who
died while squatting. That man had been a horse breaker,
but rough and brought up on the idea of force, unable to
soothe a colt even while alone in a corral. A man kicked
too often by the animals he terrified. His skull, the doctors said, had been fractured four times. The horses,
in the end, had killed him; and his brutality, however
thoughtless, had come home, his quick and rude idea—
modern and as worrisome as the idea of horses lugged
out to work in trucks with their saddles on—of how the
breaking should be done . . . slow afternoons just north
of the Black Flat barns, in the round breaking corral built
of willow thatch by the Indians from the shanties near
the creek, once Jules had possessed those afternoons.
There had been an endless future of them and he had
been young and the work of the day completed, summer forever and sure around the valley, sheltering like a
fine blue bowl. He smelled the sweating three-year-old
gelding, almost full grown and shy, with the dry and hot
odor of manure dust, and there had been only the animal
and himself and the hours before supper, time in which
a horse could be properly started without regard for the

passage of days. The animal had to be gentled firmly and slowly, brought into the bridle so it would turn with a touch on the neck and work with tenacity while understanding the obligation of its intelligence. Through all his life Jules had thought it just and proper that there had once been a people, inhabitants of what must have been a more righteous age, among whom the breaker of horses was the proudest of all men. The poet of the *Iliad* had in the final line of that poem eulogized Hector of Troy not as a prince or a warrior or a husband . . . there would be no Andromache weeping on the walls anywhere for this death . . . had remembered Hector as a breaker of horses. Jules labored through that book about conflict and pride while dust motes fell in the shafts of sunlight that patterned the oil-clean floors in the last schoolroom of his childhood. Each afternoon while other voices droned over fifth-grade fractions the tall and thin black-haired boy he had been spent an hour reading from the only printed book he could now remember, and when his father died that spring, drowning while trying to save the wagon bridge across the Mary's River south of Corvallis, his formal education and childhood ended and seemed even in the last years of his life to have given him only Hector as a model of conduct and manhood. Jules tried to tell Ambrose Vega, his boss at the Black Flat, about being remembered as a breaker of horses and could even now see the old Mexican's smile and wave of the hand, his indifference.

Vega: head man at the Black Flat Ranch before Jules was born, had come north from New Mexico with the first herds in the country. Jules saw him clearly in the breaking corral, his slow firm hands over the eyes of a black gelding, then walking away toward the cookhouse, tall with thin legs and a huge and cavernous chest from which the hollow and abrupt voice grated. "One at a time," he'd said. That chest was crushed when he died. His most trusted and experienced horse, a strong and delicate nine-year-old with a flowing long-legged stride had floundered and fallen backward while scrambling up a shale rockslide in the dry canyon above the Black Flat headquarters, and Vega had been caught between the descending tree of his saddle and a gnarled lava boulder. They sat in their own saddles and looked and waited for him to move while the frantic and ashamed horse scrambled away and the blood began to seep from Vega's mouth and nose. His stillness there on the moss-edged rock was impossible, incomprehensible. He had been old, but years from death, and they had been unable to believe he was dead or imagine the unnatural future that would follow.

At last it was Jules Russel, blind and locked into his solitary bed and cabin beneath leafless trees, young then and the educated son of a drowned veterinarian, who climbed down and saw that no one could be alive with his nose and mouth filled and bubbling with blood. For reasons he did not understand he touched his fingers to the blood and tasted the saltiness, then looked up to the figures above him on horseback and dark against the sun in the canyon stillness above the Black Flat while the body of Ambrose Vega lay on the volcanic boulder Jules was to pass innumerable times with the file of his own crew on the trail behind.

All death was no doubt quite equal, and he had been waiting for it all this last winter, really since becoming too old for horses, growing too fragile for his work. He tried to imagine the surging feel of a surefooted horse and only the clotted blanket was there, hurting his hip, and he wanted death, remembered returning for the body later that day with a yellow-brown and dog-gentle Belgian work mare wearing blinders, hauling the body down out of the canyon with the help of the man who had remained behind to keep the already-circling vultures away, loading the stiffening and blood-crusted remains of the man who had been their boss, even while old, the surest roper, who carried the work plans secretly in his head and dribbled them out each morning as if his men were children and could not be expected to remember more. The other riders went carrying the news Ambrose Vega was dead and would be kept two days in the ice-house and then buried on the sand hill back of the house, just beneath the rim of the canyon where he died.

To his burial, Jules knew, no one would bring whiskey. A man had to die on horseback and working to inspire the fear that brought men to drink as they buried. Vega had been killed in the combat of his life, and Jules knew he himself had been too careful and had outlived that sort of ceremony, lived past the importance of his life and the kind of life in which burial given the dead mattered much to those left alive. He wanted only death, and the end of disgust.

They began coming the second day, in the middle of a hot and still afternoon while whirls of dust walked over the sand hills, wagons loaded with women in long dresses and their children, the men sitting a little drunk already on the swaying seats and dressed in newly clean, patched, and homemade clothing. Lone riders, silent bitter-faced men who lived by themselves in range camps or on some dusty 160 acres of hand-cleared homestead where they were attempting to grow winter rye—land soon to be abandoned and sealed back into the desert, leaving only an eroded sand-filled cabin—began to appear out on the flat to the west, specks of black against the distant alkali whiteness of Floating Dog Lake. Those men carried rolled blankets behind their saddles and the grease-blackened leather bags hanging by the flanks of their horses occasionally clanked as earthenware jugs of whiskey knocked together. Bought with the spring supplies, and hauled out with sacks of flour and sugar and jars of hard candy in wagons on roads cut through high brush along wet-weather creeks, the whiskey was now to be used as intended, as medicine.

Toward evening Eldridge Carrier arrived. Short and white-headed and only a little past fifty, he was rich and seldom spoke. The son-in-law of a United States senator from California, he had bought three other ranches besides the Black Flat when he came north with the senator's money. His business office was in Prineville, over a hundred miles north and west in Crook County. No one knew how he learned of Ambrose Vega's death or how he came that distance so quickly. He brought his own Scotch whisky and spread his bedroll on the sand hill behind the house, away from the mosquitoes that came off the meadows, near the place where Vega was to be buried.

A fire was built up and lighted in the courtyard before the stone and rough-plank house, really just a cook shack with a few bedrooms attached. Only Vega and the cook had slept in the house. The crew bunked on straw in a shack near the barns. The firelight burned at the eyes, and Jules sat back away from it with the other men and watched the women crowding the fire with their small children, their faces burnished and excited while they talked away months of isolation. Older children ran and shouted in the darkness, playing games of pursuit in the willows marking the meadow edge. The leaf-heavy lower branches of the trees crowding the courtyard were illuminated amid flickering shadows, and as he watched their movements Jules could not stop feeling the dried crust of blood on Ambrose Vega's clothing, or smelling the dim fecund odor of the body he had lifted onto the docile and blinkered Belgian mare, the love-like odor of recent death and blood, feeling the destruction of the future . . . when a hand touched his shoulder. It was Eldridge Carrier, face unevenly lighted, hatless, and carrying a bottle of whisky. His hair appeared yellow in the light and was surprisingly long.

Carrier uncorked the bottle. "Take a swallow," he said, and his voice was so faint it might almost have been imagined. Jules sipped and handed back the bottle. "Come over to the kitchen," Carrier said. "I want to talk."

The huge room was lighted by two oil lanterns and around its perimeter, like a frieze, women rested on stools and benches, voluminous in their dresses and their faces red and blank and mostly old. They rose and fled, gathering babies and thumb-sucking grandchildren. "You can read," Carrier said. He sat the bottle on the table and gold patterns shone on the oilcloth. "In this business . . ." Carrier said, speaking after what seemed an endless time of concentration, "you can drink whisky."

"Nip on that bottle," he said. "Some men drink it all the time." Jules sipped again and knew Ambrose Vega, covered deep under damp sawdust with the stream-cut ice preserved into summer, would have kept the bottle in his hand. "You're the one that can read," Carrier said. "So you're in charge."

Those unexpected words, uttered by a man Jules then saw to be drunk, granted Jules an idea of himself he had not until then imagined. Jules saw what his life could become if he would only plan. "You send me a case of that whisky," he said. "Every month."

Carrier smiled. "That's good," he said. "I'm stuck with that." Gold teeth glittered far back in his mouth. "Now we'll see the books."

Ambrose Vega's room was stark and plain. Beneath the window was a heavy table, and on the left back corner sat a heavy strongbox, dented and showing signs of once having been painted green. Three books lay inside, bound in reddish leather worn smooth by handling. The first was titled Money, the second Numbers, and third Journal. The pages were covered with script and calculations in an elaborate hand that had no relationship to the man Jules remembered. The first book was a record of finance, the second an accounting primarily of livestock numbers, and the third a daybook recording events and accomplishments, private evaluations of men and their horses, prospects for feed and water on the desert, reasons for mistakes and their consequences. "But you can read," Carrier said. "You'll have no trouble." He stood with the bottle in his hand, slumped, his face red and greasy with sweat, and Jules understood he was to be alone and keep council only with these books. "I'll leave you the bottle," Carrier said, and he rushed from the room, slamming the door.

Jules sat leafing the pages of Ambrose Vega's private book, wondering if somewhere he would find written the secret of what he should do now. But the book revealed no private confessions. One line from the 14th of January had been crossed out with a heavy and wavering stroke of the pen. THE SNOW ALWAYS COMES FROM THE SOUTH.

Even the women were drunk at the burial. Children ran leading the procession following the board slab on which the body was carried, face exposed with dried and black rivulets of blood creasing the cheeks. The slab was too large and would not fit into the narrow, gravel-lined hole dug the evening before, and the crowd stood back from the grave and Jules was left alone in the center of their opening while they waited for someone to tip the slab and slide the body off. Then a crippled and middle-aged Indian man from the group at the back of the crowd, from the families who lived in the three shacks and beneath the willow *ramada* by the creek, came limping forward. His name was Davy Horse. He had been named after his right leg was crushed against a rock-solid juniper gatepost by a stampeding green colt he tried to ride one Sunday after-noon while he was drunk, showing off for women. Since that time he had never ridden again and vowed that he never would, and his name had evolved out of that vow. He walked everywhere he went, moving slow and broken-legged like a crab. And now Davy Horse was drunk, carry-ing a half-full bottle of dollar whiskey that he set carefully in the sand. Then he bent over the body, encircling it with his arms, lifted it and staggered sideways and fell with it into the grave. Jules was saved from an act he could never have performed. The crowd was very quiet while Jules watched Davy Horse struggle from beneath the body and then stand with one foot on a stiffened thigh, raising him-self until his shoulders were level with the ground, and si-lently lift his hand. Jules took the sweaty palm. Then Davy Horse stood above the grave and poured his whiskey over the body and into the sand, and the desert men and their women and those children who had come to the burial turned and went down the hill to their wagons and horses. The burial of Ambrose Vega was finished.

And now Jules lay alone and blind in his bed remem-bering the different man he had become. The wind had stopped, the clock was no longer ticking. He was warm and the pain in his hip was obscured by the burning in his chest. He saw the blue bowl of summer sky and his mother weeping nights after his father drowned, remembered the laughter of the small Paiute woman named Martha who cooked for him one winter in the Black Flat house, her laughter in his bed, and as he died he was weeping for the loss of an unknown woman and the children he had never allowed himself to expect, hands never touched; he could feel the tears on his face as the silence began.

The radio from Winnemucca predicted rain over the high desert of northern Nevada for the next two days. Now delicate sheets of lightning flared between the rimrocks, and the summer evening was darkened and freshened, great drops splattering into the dust and the odors of wet sage and manure mingling as the old man, Ambler, rode from the corral.

Christy was dead at twenty-three. The old man could not think about her except to see her as she had been when she was ten years old and laughing, her dark hair cropped off above her ears and her sharp face burned by the sun and wind. In the barn he had saddled the gelding quietly and mechanically, gathering the things he would need and pulling on the stiff, cold slicker, strapping the saddlebags onto the gelding and the scabbard for the thirty-thirty. Then he damped out the erratic light from the kerosene lantern and climbed into his saddle and left.

The wind came in sudden gusts, rattling the rain off his hard slicker. The rain was coming more heavily and the wind settled into a steady blow. He managed to light his pipe and settled himself into the saddle, smelling the aroma of the rough-cut tobacco and seeing only the small glow of the pipe.

There was a fence and then a gate, and the old man got down and led the gelding through and then set off on a pair of narrow wagon tracks that led directly away from the fence. The tracks curved up gently through the rising sand hills on an old trail tramped by the antelope and mustangs and Paiutes. Finally the horse began to climb, stumbling in the gravel and rock where the wagon tracks had been eroded into small gullies. Ambler could smell the sour wet mahogany brush that grew in clumps under the rimrocks, and then the land leveled out and he pulled the horse in and rested sideways in the saddle, easing himself.

Far out below he could see the first glimmerings of light from the house, light from the uncurtained windows flickering through what he knew were the leaves of the long row of Lombardy poplar trees. The wagon track came out on a new road, and fresh gravel crunched under the hooves of the gelding. About a hundred yards from the house there was a lull in the wind, a silence, and then a half-dozen hounds came baying and yelping toward him. The old man clapped the romal on the tree of his saddle and sent the gelding leaping forward, and then just short of the fence he jerked the horse up and was off him, talking to the animal, soothing him while the dogs yipped.

The front door to the house opened. The man in the doorway shouted once at the dogs and sent them around the corner of the house. The only sounds now were the hum of the Delco power plant and splatter of rain and wind. The tall young man came from out of the doorway, far enough to see who it was. "Jesus Christ, Walt," he said.

Old Man Ambler had the gelding under control and stepped forward, leading him easily by the reins. "Hello, Barry," he said. "Christy died yesterday."

"What are you talking about? Let's put that horse away."

They bedded the horse in the small slope-roofed shed that passed as a barn. When they were through, the boy stopped in the doorway of the shed, looking across the lot toward the house. He lighted a cigarette. "What about Christy?" he said finally.

"I need a place to sleep," the old man said.

"There's nobody in Eddie's room. He went to town a week ago and ain't got enough of it to suit him yet. Sooner or later I'll have to go get him."

They went across the muddy lot toward the house, toward the light that gleamed across the puddles. Inside the back screen door the young man helped Ambler out of his slicker and chaps and hung them on pegs along the back wall. Sitting outside in the rain were three nearly new cars and an old pickup truck with the side windows knocked out.

Going into the light and warmth of the kitchen, Ambler was blinded momentarily. The youngest of the brothers, the young man who'd been helping him, said, "Guess you know everybody, Walt."

"Close enough," Ambler said, and he did, remembered all of them, the three brothers and the missing one. Even the old hired man, he remembered him from someplace. The eldest of them, John, who ran the business, got up and waved him to a seat in front of the oil stove and took his mackinaw coat and said, "Sit and warm yourself. Nora can get you coffee and a plate of food."

Three women sat around the room, two young ones who were knitting and the old woman, Nora, the mother of the boys. Ambler nodded at each of them in turn and then sat in front of the stove. The older woman got up and went to the stove where she filled a plate with meat and potatoes leftover from the evening meal.

One of the boys had been playing a guitar. He stopped

and let his fingers run softly over the strings. Grinning uneasily, he slapped his hands on the box of the instrument and moved it to hang it on the wall. "Too much static for the radio," he said. The sound of the wind was muted inside the building, but Ambler could hear it as he ate and the family silently watched.

"Maybe you wonder why I come over here all of a sudden," the old man said, when he had handed his plate back to the woman. "Six years since I come into this house the last time. I was going to kill Eddie. Tonight I had the same idea. What happened was Christy got killed Saturday night. She never come home from the time she run off with Eddie. But now it's all done with and I want you people to know I don't care anymore, and to finish this off with no more trouble." The old man lit his pipe again when he was through talking, staring down into the bowl while he worked at it.

"We got no manners." The oldest brother dug into the cupboard under the sink, and came up with a half-full bottle of bourbon. One of the young women put five heavy glass tumblers on the table. After his drink the hired man rose without speaking and went off upstairs and could be heard moving around his room and then dropping his boots and rolling into bed. The eldest son showed old man Ambler to his room—an unpainted and unadorned place above the stairs.

"We're all sorry she's dead, Walt." The man spoke quietly. He had his hand on the doorknob and was half in and half out of the room. "She was the best there was around here, Walt, but I can't see where it was Eddie that spoiled her."

The old man sat on the bed. "Maybe not."

"Could be you set her up higher than she was. Just

the two of you for so long." The man, Eddie's brother, closed the door and left Ambler alone in the room.

The old man heaped his things onto a chair and dropped his boots among the scattered gear of the absent younger son who had six years ago run off with Christy and then dumped her completely when the sheriff brought them back from Reno after three weeks. The old man pulled the string on the single bare lightbulb and was surprised the radium-dial alarm clock showed the time to be after midnight.

Lying quiet he was aware of the drumming of the rain that was being driven against the slanting roof above him. *Dead*, he thought. She has known everything for these last two days. He turned in the bed of the boy who had started her and wondered how it had been in the light and sharp-edged shadows out in the dust and tumbleweeds where the cars were parked around a country dance hall two hundred miles away, over near the foot of the Ruby Mountains. She had been shot square in the chest and dead before anyone knew better in a fight between two unknown drunken men. The pretty girl with the long black hair dead when they reached her—the deputy sheriff hung his head and told the story through once and then left, the dust from his going rising high in an alkali-colored rooster tail hanging far off in the afternoon stillness before the storm. Ambler stared at the raftered darkness and wished luck to the stranger who would dope out so many years in the state penitentiary for killing her, wished she could have been home just once lately, and wondered if he would have killed Eddie Matson with the thirty-thirty when it came right down to it. He tried to remember her and wished he had a photo of her taken in these last years because all he could remember was the long swinging hair tied with a red ribbon the last time she visited, and the pointed face of the little girl. He slept then, lulled by the whiskey and already sick of his own despair.

In the morning he ate with them, saddled the gelding, and rode off, his yellow slicker outlining him against the sage hills in rain. The rain soaked his hat and the brim drooped before his face. Water dropped in steady streams from the horse's mane. The animal kept its head down and picked easily through the natural paths in the sagebrush, plodding heavily. Far off through the sweeping slants of the storm the horizon lay flat with steps of rimrock in some places, but mostly he watched close beside the path the horse picked and saw the straggling grass that grew among the rocks was already greener. The feed would hold for the rest of the dry season. There was no wind. Dropping the reins over the saddle horn, he stuffed his hands into the pocket of his slicker. The horse continued to choose its own way.

At the rim of the canyon, Ambler climbed off. This trail was dangerous when dry and worse now, and there could be no reason to cripple a horse over this sort of foolishness. So the two of them slipped and stumbled down the trail until they were at the bottom of the dry prehistoric river course, working upstream toward the cave and the spring. Around the little waterhole were a few scrub willow, and at the mouth of the cave, where the tiny stream came into daylight, the old man saw signs of watering livestock along with antelope and mule-deer signs. Wild horses had used this hidden water until after the war, when they were run with airplanes and slaughtered for dog food.

The cave was broad as a large room. When the old man had unsaddled the gelding he hauled the saddle and bed into the mouth of the shelter and unrolled his tarp. He hobbled the horse in a sheltered place in the willows. Ambler smoked and made up his mind how to go about this last piece of business.

As the afternoon darkened he went down to the spring and drank and then went back to the bedroll and dug out a sack of dried venison jerky and cut slivers with his knife and munched slowly while the gray daylight faded into evening. The cave extended far into the darkness behind him and he could smell the warm and acrid odor of nesting animals, and hear the rustling of mice and squirrels and hear the dripping of the water that gathered to form the little spring. When he could no longer see, he pulled off his boots and climbed between the rough blankets and slept.

The bar was crowded two deep along the rail, and he edged through until the barkeep poured him a shot and scooped up his two bits. All through the crowd were riders with numbers pinned to the backs of their bright shirts.

Another drink. He sipped it slowly, quiet amid the ungainly and brawny women and the somber toothpick-chewing men, then worked his way back to the sidewalk. Taking his key at the hotel desk he went up to his room, stopped before the door, and knocked. No answer. She was not there. On the bare frame dresser he found a note telling him she had gone downstairs to the coffee shop.

He lay on the bed, his feet propped over the end, his eyes wandering over the stark room. The woman had not settled anything. He rolled off the bed and walked to the window and leaned with his hands against the sill while he watched the crowd on the street. Men fished in their pockets for cigarette materials, their faces working and squinting while they talked, a line of gossiping country men with their feet propped on the high bumpers of beaten cars, pickups. Another group of men stood beside the entrance to the hotel—ranchers with cigars and engraved belts and business voices. The hot-dog stand at the corner was surrounded with women and children. He watched them and looked for some clue to whatever mystery he was contemplating. Then he heard his new bride outside in the hallway, her quiet voice coming clearly through the transom.

Christy was dead.

Her mother: black hair and pale body bent as she watched herself in some long bedroom mirror, her ribs showing through the flesh, and the thing that fascinated him, the winding of the long hair in the tight coil she made for sleeping. And then the birth, their only child. The woman had lain awake at night beside him and taken to disregarding him. Then she rode off in the middle of a summer day, on the best saddle mare he ever owned, leaving the seven-year-old girl for him to discover in the evening light, sitting on the front steps and waiting.

Ambler was awake. The rain had stopped. To the east there was a strip of clear and intense blue sky between the horizon and the layer of clouds. His horse was off cropping grass below the water hole. The grass and sage were heavy with moisture, and the air was chilled and fresh.

After a while Ambler sat up and pulled on his boots, shivering. He ate more of the jerky. Then he went out and caught the horse and pulled off the hobbles and sent the startled animal off at a run with a slap on its haunches.

Back in the cave he loaded the thirty-thirty, wondering while he did it if he should wash himself or at least clean his mouth with some of the springwater, and then he thought to hell with it and wondered if he should pray or something and then laughed at himself.

Maybe these things are not enough, he thought, and he lifted the thirty-thirty, weighing it in his grasp, a relic of older and better times. As he laid the rifle on the bed-roll a glint of dark white back in the shadows of the cave caught his eye. It was the skull of a badger, lying among remnants of bone and hide, picked clean by the mice and ants and identifiable only by the scrap of fur.

Ambler examined the tiny and delicate structure of the bones in the skull as though it were something never seen before and looked closely at the way the teeth were fastened to the jawbone, built for hanging on. You are a hapless fool, he thought, and unloaded the rifle and rolled it inside the bedroll. He heaped his possessions on a ledge inside the cave and began the long walk home.

It was evening of the second day before he reached the home place. The gelding was waiting for him, cropping grass outside the first gate. The sun had set and all around him were the quiet movements of small animals. The old man fixed himself a meal and watched the air outside his windows darken and cool. He went to bed and slept. Then for no reason other than the rasping of his own breath, he was awake and opening his eyes to the board wall. He turned in the bed, thinking he would be awake now and unable to sleep, but even while turning notic-ing the oddness. The window across the room was light from the moon, and around the window there was the deep and solid yellow light, and as he saw it there was a compelling sensation of *person*—some other thing shar-ing the room with him.

Without surprise he saw a figure leaning against the wall, regarding him, and then it turned to the window. For a moment in the moonlight there was a face silhouetted, a profile of someone who he might have known, once, no ghost but a face he could almost catch a name for, a haggard woman, and then it was gone and Ambler felt it all slipping away, like something dreamed. *Who is this?* he thought.

The old man sank in the bed and turned to face the wall and wondered whatever had happened to him, or tried to happen, what thing had been revealed that he could not understand or feel anything toward except revulsion. He could not remember the face, just that he had seen a face, and some terrible nervousness of energy was trembling through him.

The rest of the night he lay awake. Toward daybreak he rose and built a fire in the kitchen and made coffee and drank it heavy with sugar and condensed milk. It was warm and it helped calm him. Finally he made breakfast, venison steak and milk gravy, and after eating he cleaned the dishes and went to sit in one of the big chairs in the main room of the house, chairs he had hauled in from Elko, bought at auction after the old Sheepman Hotel closed. With the full light of day he could recall little of the experience of the night before, only that it had happened.

For a long time he didn't work away from the house and the corrals, the barn and his small meadows. He worked slowly at the business of stockpiling his hay down by the windmill and in the barn loft. As the days passed at the slow tasks, working alone as he always had, Ambler tried to recapture what had happened that night in the moonlight.

The summer began to fade and finally it was fall. He

rode out into the desert because it was necessary, and pushed his cattle in toward the meadows so when the snow came they would be home. Some days he worked in the barn, getting ready for winter, mending harness and building new side racks for the sled he used for feeding when the snow was down.

From the loft of the barn, looking east, breaking loose the mud-dauber sparrows' nests with a shovel handle, Ambler saw the bareheaded horseman climbing down to open the last gate. Ambler watched the man close the wire gate, and saw who it was, Eddie Matson, the boy who had run off with Christy those years ago. The only annoyance Ambler felt was at the interruption of his solitude—just like a kid to be riding this desert country without a hat, a red bandanna tied around his forehead and draped down over his neck in the back as some kind of defense against the sun, which was, after all, in this fall season, no longer strong enough to bother.

But Eddie Matson was no longer a kid, he was unshaven and a man and close to thiry years old as Ambler looked up at him after climbing down from the barn loft. Whatever could be wrong with Eddie Matson was wrong. His eyes were mattering and squinted, like he had not slept, and his shotgun horsehide chaps were out at the knees, worn through. Eddie Matson sucked at his lower lip, like he was tasting the feel of his whiskers. "By God," he said, "here I am."

Ambler nodded, but didn't answer, only walked off toward the house, listening to the slow footfalls of Eddie Matson's gelding as it followed. Ambler turned. "How long you been riding that horse? You had better turn him loose for a rest. There's oats in the saddle shed."

Inside the house, Ambler reheated the morning coffee

and set out two cups and poured whiskey into each, while Eddie Matson watched. "You can sleep the night," Ambler said, "and rest that horse, and then you might as well be gone."

Only after they had finished the coffee, after Ambler had fried some bacon while Eddie Matson drank another cup of coffee, as Eddie chewed at his thick sandwich, the bacon between thick slices of bread, did they do any talking, and then it was Ambler who got it started. "You can break your ass on these things," he said, "once you get it going."

Eddie Matson nodded. "A number of things," he said. "You just run out of speed. Things go as far as they can go, and then they don't go anymore."

"That's the truth, far as it carries. You tell me what you come here for."

Eddie Matson chewed at another mouthful, and wiped his mouth with the back of his hand. "That's hard to say. Just to say I'm sorry about Christy, but I never thought you were right. We went down to Reno, them deputies come and took her home. I never come to get her again, she wouldn't have stayed with me either, you know that, she never stayed here with you after that, much. You figure that's my fault, but I don't see it." With a cupped hand Eddie Matson brushed crumbs from the flowered oilcloth on the table, and looked across at Ambler, slate-colored eyes deep in themselves and intent on saying a thing that Eddie couldn't excuse himself from trying to say, which had to be most of why he was here. "She started herself—there is nobody else to blame."

"Sounds to me like you are making excuses for yourself," Ambler said. "We can all make excuses and do things we hate, and if there's one thing, it's to quit doing that. I scared the piss out of myself awhile back, it was

nobody but me, and maybe now I have quit doing everything, but I've tried to quit doing things I hate." This talk,
as it came from him, was forming, and Ambler wondered
how much he meant what he was saying as he listened
to himself, and what he had quit doing beyond trusting
his nerve.

"Make you a deal," Ambler said. Eddie Matson looked
away, and just shook his head, as if yes, there should
be a deal. "You come live here on this place, when you
think you can." Ambler wondered what it was he was
offering.

Eddie Matson kept nodding yes, and looked back at
Ambler, and this time his eyes had gone surface gray
again. "You getting too old?"

Ambler got up and poured them both more of the
bitter coffee, and more of the whiskey that stood on the
table between them. "Not so much that as give out with
it all."

"Soon as I get a chance," Eddie Matson said. "All right.
There are things that could be done around here."

But there was never a chance. The last week in October the wind blew cold from the north, and the Indian
summer was over and always the first thing Ambler did
those days when he came in from work was stoke up the
fire and thaw out. There were only a few days of sleet rain
before the gray November day when the snow began to
come down in the late afternoon. Ambler watched it and
remembered his daughter.

She had followed him across the slippery meadows
and he had taken her hand and helped her keep up while
the half circles of dampness on the worn toes of her boots
grew larger and she laughed and puffed in the frosty air
and they watched her breath float away. There seemed
too much of himself in these memories. He wondered if

he was, as they had said, too much taken up with her, and then he thought to hell with them.

The next morning the new dry snow covered the ground and was falling straight and soft in absolute stillness. In the evening he got up from his chair exhausted, surprised to realize he had not eaten and must be hungry. He forced himself to build a fire and cooked a steak and baked potato and mixed gray milk gravy and cut bread, and then he sat down and ate slowly. When he finished eating he was warm and at peace, and he smoked and looked out to where the little creek that flowed in front of the house was carving through the new drifts. The spring will come early, he thought, and the feed will be good. I'll turn out early and go spend some time in town. With drowsiness softening his thoughts, he started toward the bedroom when he fell and lay two hours unconscious before he started to drag himself somewhere, and then he was dead, of natural causes.

They didn't discover him until Eddie Matson finally came along and found his few head of starving cattle walking the fence line and gnawing the posts. After some search they located the widow and she had the place sold at auction. It went to a feedlot outfit from the Sacramento Valley in California, who were buying up land with water all along the western foothills of the Steens Mountains for summer range. Eddie Matson leased the house and lived there alone seven years, until he married one of the Lamar sisters from Bonanza and moved over near Klamath Falls. He always said, living out his later years (on the dairy farm his wife inherited), that Old Man Ambler had taught him one thing, although it was hard to name. Something like never looking to see the time of day, never owning a watch, always guessing by the look of the sun. And night, he said, and he laughed, night didn't count.

1

A new world every morning. Every night, Banta thought, every time the sun turns sideways. *Rock of ages, near to thee,* crooning through the static from the Hallicrafter radio, voices in rising harmony while the postcard scenes of his life hung on another slope, his bluebird mornings slipped away, back into the white noise that scratched with the music.

So now Grace was dead, and Danzig was dead, and they all were dead. Someone would have to clean up the mess. But not me, Banta thought. Banta stood with his hands on the cold enamel rim of the kitchen sink, studying the elongated shadows of light cast out from the windows. They lay soft as reflections of a summer moon on the new snow.

Sparks from the exhaust of the pumping, diesel-fueled electric generator fanned away into the twilight like midwinter fireflies. Banta dug a yellow stocking cap from the pocket of his sheepskin coat, and orange-tinted skier's goggles, and went out into the cold where he tightened the cinch around the belly of his black gelding. Then he climbed up into the saddle and rode away.

How to stay alive in the snowy woods—old lessons. *Avoid panic. Think of taking hostages.* Virgil Banta rode an unplowed lane between bare-limbed cottonwoods and across the echoing bridge above Marshall Creek, down

153

toward the Clark Fork of the Columbia and the high-way. The snow fell steadily, as it had since the third day after Christmas, large fragile flakes dropping through the windless cold.

Do not be afraid of telling lies. Remember that, remember this, remember every detail, every step of this way. In the snowy woods. Instructions from Danzig. But Danzig was dead.

Just down the hill from the fence where Danzig lay frozen half-under the snow, Virgil Banta climbed from the gelding. Banta thought of Danzig frozen, those strong white fingers stiff enough to break clean off like sticks if you hit them with a hammer. Danzig had been plow-ing the road in from the highway when he died. When Banta shot him. The angle-bladed cable-drum old D7 Caterpillar was a dark shadow up in the jack pine where it stalled after Danzig fell off the seat, dead. Banta opened his pants and stood pissing, his blood-stiff yellow buckskin gloves tucked under one arm. When he finished, standing over the steaming hole in the snow, he picked for a mo-ment at the frozen clotted blood with a thumbnail, tossed the gloves into a thicket of buckbrush below the road, and climbed on the gelding once more, settling into the skiff of snow already feathering on the seat of his high-forked saddle.

When Virgil Banta reached the highway along the river, and night settled into the steep-walled canyon, two does and a forked-horn buck came to lick at the salty yellow stain where he had pissed. In the brushy thicket a porcupine began to gnaw at the bloody gloves.

Another slope of his life. The year Virgil was ten and his sister Grace was eight, that summer their friend Skinny Burton died of drowning, his sharp-ribbed body white and limp in red bathing trunks on the grass between two willow-tree stumps. A Sunday afternoon, and their father crouched over Skinny, pumping at his chest, while a thin dribble of water ran from Skinny's nose, but Skinny was dead.

Grace stayed to watch. Virgil ran and hid in the cool meathouse where blocks of creek-ice survived in the summer under wet sawdust. Virgil chipped slivers off the ice and sucked them. The dim interior of that insulated building was very quiet. His only visitor was a calico mouse-hunting cat.

That night on the screened-in veranda overlooking the valley of the Bitterroot River, he asked his mother if dead people cry. "No," his mother said, her arm heavy around his shoulder, "your grandmother didn't cry when she was dying."

Virgil could remember the endless raspy voice of his grandmother singing unintelligible wheezing verses of some song from her childhood in the back bedroom before she died. Lights from the other ranches out in the shadowland of meadow and willow where Virgil was a child, those lights flickered as they shone through the screen around the porch. Virgil could make them flicker by moving his head. His father came home from the funeral parlor in Hamilton, where Skinny Burton was being drained of creekwater and his blood, and dressed and rouged to look the way he looked three days later in an open coffin. The dull red GMC pickup rattled over the cattle-guard by the barn and stopped just short of the porch, nosing into the light. His father looked old and tired as he stood in the kitchen sipping coffee and smelling of whiskey.

"How could he cry?" Grace said later, sitting up on her bed in their attic bedroom where frost would form on the rafters in wintertime. She had long braids, and her face was scrubbed and gleaming under the single bulb dangling from the ridgepole. "He was under the water."

Under the water, Banta thought.

Virgil lay quiet that night after Grace was asleep and listened to her breathe. He wondered what it would be like dying under the water, looking up to the light. And now Grace was dead, and she *had* cried—there had been tears on her face when she died. Grace was dead, and Danzig was dead, and up there in the house they were all dead, and he'd killed them.

The storms came in from the Pacific, over the Cascades and the flatland wheatfields of eastern Washington. All his life Shirley Holland had watched them come over the Bitterroot Mountains to play out and dump themselves in Montana, snow falling in the soft wind that blew flakes down the streets like dust. It was like the coming and going of seawater. Like the drift of tide.

In the kitchen, under the sink with the bottles of bleach and ammonia, there was an unopened bottle of Sunnybrook. Shirley Holland bought Sunnybrook because he liked the name. Carefully he cut the plastic seal with the tip of his knife and poured a couple of inches into a water glass, the whiskey glowing amber like fishing water in the late days of fall. *A new world every morning.* He had been a young man then, the third year he was sheriff, when he hired a traveling sign painter to print those words in three-foot-high letters across the outside wall of his cinder-block jailhouse. It was something he learned from his father. The old man had been talking about drunks locked in the tank to sober up overnight, and about himself when he got old and couldn't remember the seasons. In old age his father had lived by himself, and said he sometimes woke in the morning and looked out expecting to see snow and found himself surprised by blossoming lilac. You would think a man would know, his father said, just by the light. His voice trailed off, and he stared at the wall as if amazed to discover such a fool in himself. The old man hadn't sympathy for drunks, even when he was drinking himself. Shirley Holland thought of those words every time he started at the whiskey. *A new world every morning.* Faded words lettered on the side of his jailhouse like a motto for his life.

Shirley Holland was at his kitchen table, sipping his second glass of whiskey, when someone pounded at the living-room door. "Doris," he said, "tell them to go across the street and see Billy."

But after she mumbled to whoever it was, Doris came scuffing down the hallway toward him in her buckskin slippers. "Holland," she said, "you better come out here."

"Tell them I'm not in business," Shirley Holland said.

Doris chewed at her upper lip, staring at her reflection in the dark window over the sink. "The thing is," she said, "he looks exactly like you." She glanced toward Holland, one of her quick old-time looks, part grin, that took him back to the barroom years when they courted and ran together before they were married. Maybe this was another shot at what she had taken to talking about as her joking. Just this last year she had gone distant and strange on him. After sixteen years, this woman with her rimless school-teacher eyeglasses and her blond hair going thin and gray now, had gone away from him. On Christmas day, spooning oyster dressing out of their turkey, just the two of them because there hadn't been any children—she didn't want children growing up in a sheriff's house was her excuse for having her tubes tied off—she started talking about a song she heard on the radio, a song called "Satan's

Jewel Crown." Doris said it made her think about those people out there who were courting the devil by cutting the tongues and privates out of dead cows and leaving the rest. She said the song made her sad because no one ever offered to ruin her life, and she said she was thinking about spending the spring in San Francisco.

"Even Coit Tower," she said. "I never even been to Coit Tower. I would have gone with a woman even. If she'd asked me." Holland hadn't answered, just took himself a helping of string beans and let it drop. That night, looking up from a fancy picture book about the lives of French kings, she said it was a joke. "That part about a woman in San Francisco, anyway," she said, "that was a joke." "Funny as hell," Shirley Holland said, and she looked at him and shook her head.

Now, someone waiting at the front door, she was shaking her head again, like Holland was responsible for terrible sadness everywhere, like she could cry.

"Looks the spitting image of you," she said.

"Only maybe," she said, and out of her sadness she grinned, "he might be left-handed."

The kid didn't look anything like him, just some big-shouldered kid, maybe twenty years old, wearing a yellow knit skier's cap, with ice and snow in his long hair and beard, but a working kid from the looks of his hands. But then maybe Doris wasn't joking. The kid looked like the son of somebody Holland had known.

"There is trouble," the kid said in a flat voice, as though it was nothing of much consequence. "Out to that Danzig house up there on Marshall Creek."

"There ain't no Danzig house," Shirley Holland said. "You mean the Frantz place."

"The place that Danzig fellow leased," the kid said.

"There sure as hell is something wrong out there," Shirley Holland said. "You one of them?"

"My sister was Grace. My name is Virgil Banta. You knew my father. He was Mac Banta."

The kid pulled off his yellow stocking cap. His eyes were dark points in the dim entryway light. "There has been a crowd of people killed," he said.

"My sister," he said, "they killed Grace." Shirley Holland wondered what to do with this, as he watched the kid's eyes fill with tears. It was like watching an animal begin to weep.

The inside of the four-wheel-drive Chevrolet pickup cab was warm enough. The wipers were swiping and the heater was blowing hot air out the defroster vents and onto his hands, and the air smelled of tobacco and sweaty clothing. But every twenty or so minutes Shirley Holland would have to stop and let the deputy, Billy Kumar, get out and break the ice off the wipers, and then Holland would feel the brittle midnight cold. Billy would get back inside with snow on his red and black timber-cruiser jacket and everything would stink a little worse of damp wool, like drowned sheep.

"It's the bombs," Billy Kumar said, talking about the weather. "Every time they set off another of them nuclear bombs."

Shirley Holland chewed at a matchstick. His shoulders ached. The ruts in the road were frozen hard, and the pickup rocked and churned, the steering wheel bucking in his hands. Almost half a lifetime of herding drunks, watching while some mechanic with a cutting torch released the body of another drunk from the crushed interior of an old car, or maybe a woman shotgunned while she was sleeping in bed. One whiskey-stinking wreck or bedroom after another, and then a long afternoon in the office, typing up reports. And now this deputy, Billy Kumar, dumber than rocks and talking about bombs.

"Never been the same," Billy Kumar said gesturing quickly with the left hand where he wore a heavy silver ring with a setting of polished green opal. Billy held his buff-colored Stetson between his knees and fingered endlessly at the band, turning the hat counterclockwise as he did.

"Where did you get that ring?" Shirley Holland asked.

"Last year in Las Vegas."

"Makes you look like a queer."

Billy Kumar didn't answer. Maybe it *was* the bombs, Holland mused. Snow before Thanksgiving, and then right before Christmas, days of spring-like thaw and flooding, bridges washing out, and now this week of blizzard. At least they were not out here on horseback, freezing their asses. They were only a little more than a mile from the house. In the old days the place had been run as a hunting camp. This was before Amos Frantz died and his property sold. Hunting camp and part-time whorehouse. Since then there hadn't been any sort of hunting camp. In the old days there weren't any of these rich people playing at make-believe, dressing up in Indian costumes and riding snowmobiles. "There's gamblers in Las Vegas wearing rings like this," Billy Kumar said, "and nobody better call them queers."

They were right at the fence the kid had talked about, just down from where that D7 Cat was stalled up on the hillside in the jack pines. The canyon sloped up out of the headlights on that side, and to the right was the darkness that was the wash of Marshall Creek. From here the road wouldn't be even half plowed. "Billy," Holland said, "you take a rest. You wait for me right here."

After tying one of Doris's old nylon stockings over his ears like a headband and pulling his stockman's hat down, Holland stepped out into fluffy new snow that was knee deep over the old frozen crust, and started climbing toward the dark shadow of that D7 Caterpillar. The hillside was so steep it looked as if the machine might, if somebody only touched it, rock and turn slowly and come thundering down. But the question was: what the hell was it doing there?

Holland was resting with his hands on his knees, out of wind, head down and dizzy, and thought maybe it was something he imagined when he heard Billy Kumar shout. Then another shout, muffled and echoing, and frightened, and he knew it was Billy. The deputy had turned over the frozen, snowy body of a dead man. "You didn't see him, did you?" Billy said. "There was an arm sticking up. I saw it plain as hell. God Almighty."

The damned fool, Shirley Holland thought. Now we've got this, and he's got himself scared shitless. Billy had jerked on the arm and found he had hold of a frozen hand, and he'd fallen backward. He stood there covered with snow and looking frightened enough to cry. Shirley Holland knelt beside the body and brushed the snow from the face.

"One of them kids," he said, but it wasn't a kid at all. He brushed more snow from the face. This was Danzig, a fifty-year-old man, features distorted in the lights from the pickup reflecting off the snow, just a thin face and long hair iced into thick brittle strands. Shirley Holland kept brushing away the snow and then stopped. This dead man, whose features he was polishing like stone, had been shot, the bullet entering in a neat small high-velocity hole just in front of and above the right ear and passing out through the back of the neck, leaving a jagged frozen wound the size of a teacup. The hard flesh was rough as wood to the touch, the mouth half closed on a twisted upper plate, and the eyes turned up, open and blank, frosted white.

There was nothing to say. Billy Kumar made a move like he was going to run, but held his ground. "Get hold of his feet," Holland said. "I'll take the head."

"You think so?" Billy Kumar said. "You think we ought to move him right away?"

"Yeah," Shirley Holland said, "we ought to move him."

The body was frozen sprawled, arms and legs spread like a starfish. Holland dropped his end twice before they reached the pickup. His chest ached, and his hands didn't have any feeling. "You ain't even thirty years old," Shirley said, "so don't be looking at me. You just lift him over the tailgate, else we are going to be here all night."

With his eyes closed, Billy got hold of the body, arms around the dead man's waist. The snow-covered steel flooring of the pickup bed echoed dully when they dropped the frozen body inside. They warmed themselves in the pickup cab, and Billy turned the radio to country music. Roger Miller singing, *Trailer for sale or rent*. Shirley wanted to laugh. How long since he had heard that song? There had been a night drinking and dancing with whatever women were around when they had played that song over and over. He never noticed when songs went off the jukebox. Back around 1965, at least that far back. "If I'm going to concentrate," Holland said, "you are going to shut that off."

Why concentrate? The thing to do was go back for help. But that didn't feel right. The kid was there with

Doris. "You don't leave town," he had told the kid. "He can stay here," Doris said. "I'll fix some bacon and some eggs. Just like home." The kid had wiped the tears out of his eyes and smiled at her.

"There is a ghost up here," Shirley Holland said to Billy Kumar. The pickup was plowing two or so feet of dry snow, but not lurching in the ruts the way it had. "There's a ghost of a dead Chinaman."

When he was eleven or twelve, the first of the hunting campouts his father had trusted him with, the men had told him a story about a Chinese camp cook who died and had been buried in the foundation of the house. "We rocked him up under the south corner," his father said, "to keep the coyotes away. The next spring he was dried up and there was no smell at all."

"Under there," his father said, showing him the rock pile against the southeast corner of the house. "His bones are under there yet if his people ain't come for him. Them people believe in things like that, ghosts coming for your bones."

Billy Kumar was fingering his hatband again. "There ain't no ghosts," Shirley Holland said, "no more than there are ghosts of cows."

In an upstairs bedroom Amos Frantz kept a whore from Butte whose name was Linda. She stayed most of one hunting season, and her feet had been caked with dirt as she cried and waved all the way across the bridge when Amos put her gear into his pickup and hauled her down the canyon and back to the Bluebird House in Butte. Flakes of snow lifted in the headlights like floating goose down. No ghosts at all.

One drunken night Holland had pissed into the fireplace, onto the burning cedar coals, up there in that house. Holland had been sleeping in the living room, and the snapping coals had kept him awake, and he had been trying to put them out while listening to the mumbled cursing of the other men bedded in the room. The stink of that scorching urine was with him now. The sandstone mantel over the fireplace had been darkened by soot over the years, and the next morning they had all carved their initials into the soft rock. Shirley Holland had carved an S H inside a heart.

Out in the clouding snow the house hovered like some lighted craft coming toward them, the glow diffusing into lapping auras in the falling snow, silt stippling the darkness. Shirley Holland refused to take the pickup across the bridge above Marshall Creek. "We'll walk it," he said. "Slide a wheel off that thing, and there you'll be."

Billy Kumar reached to lift the sawed-off 12-gauge shotgun from the rack behind the pickup seat. "You ain't going to need that," Shirley Holland said. "There ain't going to be anybody up there. The kid said there was nobody alive in there, and if there is they will shoot us while we're walking."

"Or be glad to see us," Holland said, reaching under the pickup seat for the bottle of Sunnybrook. "There's some of them people would be glad to see anybody."

Doris Holland was playing religious music from a Christmas album of four long-playing records, the only church music in the house. The *Messiah*. The long-haired boy, his name was Virgil Banta, wanted to hear something good for the soul. That was what he said, good for the soul. He was sitting cross-legged on the floor beside the record player, wearing an old flannel shirt of Holland's that almost fit. Just a little short in the sleeves. Doris had given him the shirt when he came out of the shower. She knocked at the door of the steamy bathroom to tell him the omelet was ready, with warmed-over lima beans and remnants of ham hocks on the side, and he had come out with no shirt on, rubbing his long hair with a towel, and his chest at least as furry as Holland's. She turned away and got him the washed-out shirt from Holland's chest of drawers.

Poor child with his sister dead. Doris had a brother, who was dead. Doris could still see her brother's rouged face turned up at the whitewashed rafters of the Methodist church in Elk River, Idaho. All the people who had been there she hadn't seen for a long time—Dora and Slipper Count, small as wrinkled children in their seventies, hands shaking because they lived every day but Sunday on wine; and Marly Prester and his new wife; and the others, Old Man Duncan Avery and all those children.

The music stopped and the boy went on staring at his bare feet. Doris got up to turn the records and he stopped her. "That's not the music," he said.

"How come you want me to look like him?" the boy said.

"I don't want you to, you just do."

"That's your idea," he said.

His eyes were gray, the same as Holland's. "You fit his shirt," Doris said.

"Well, that about gets it," he said. "That's about all of his I would fit." He looked up and smiled slowly, like he had forgotten his sister was dead.

"How do you know that?" she said.

"Your feet get cold," he said, "you put on your hat. That's the rule. Your head is like a refrigerator, you have to turn it off to get your fingers and toes warm. So you put on your hat.

"That's rule number eleven," he said. "Danzig taught me that rule." He got up and went into the hallway where his yellow stocking cap was stuffed into the pocket of his sheepskin coat. He pulled the cap down over his wet hair. "Now," he said, "I don't feel no pain, because my head is covered.

"You got to do lots of things this way," he said, "with your head turned off. Danzig taught me all that. And how to stay alive." The boy laughed, and pulled off the stocking cap. "But now Danzig is dead," he said.

"You aren't like Holland at all," Doris said. "You only look like Holland, that's all."

"You'll get used to it," Virgil Banta said, sitting down on the floor again, this time right in front of where she sat on the couch. "Don't you think so?" he said. "I got used to Danzig. For a long time I was used to Danzig. But now Danzig is dead, and after a while they'll get me."

"I guess that doesn't make any sense," Doris said, holding herself very quiet because he was touching her foot, easing the slipper off her right foot and starting his fingers working softly between her toes. No, there was nothing in him that was at all like Holland, she thought. Poor child with a dead sister. It was important to keep knowing he was a poor child with a dead sister, and nothing around him but this house.

2

Seven orange backpacks, fully loaded, right down to tightly rolled sleeping bags, were lined along the far wall. The orange contrasted vividly against the sea green wallpaper, and splattered across the orange nylon there was a spray of dried blood. But it wasn't the blood that surprised Shirley Holland, it was the warmth of the house, propane heat and the neatness of everything but the bodies. *Blown away*, Shirley Holland thought, *milk in the pudding.* Words of a song he'd known as a child. What could they mean now? The walls had been torn out so the ground floor was one room, including the kitchen, and there was the hardware: seven sets of binoculars on a dark table against the wall beside the packboards, seven leather cases that must contain binoculars. And the automatic rifles, Holland recognized them from pictures, leaning one by one alongside the packboards. And above all that, a slogan painted high on the green wall: THE SEVEN DWARFS. Each end of the room was decorated with a huge black-and-white poster, one of Ché Guevara and one of Chairman Mao. And there was a television set silently playing. The picture on the television set was the only thing moving. Shirley Holland turned away. "You best go wait in the pickup," he said to Billy Kumar, who was behind him on the entry porch.

"What if there is somebody?" Billy Kumar said.

"There ain't going to be nobody, at least nobody that ought to get us excited." Which was the old secret, do not get excited, look around and make sense of things, count the holes and think of reasons why. "There is not going to be a damned soul around here, soon as you go outside and turn off that television set." Shirley Holland turned to find Billy Kumar's short-barreled Detective Special .38 automatic aimed dead into his back.

"Billy," Shirley Holland said, "you might shoot me, and then where would we be? You go sit on the front steps." He figured Billy might drive off if he got near the pickup. "You just put that gun away and take a rest," Shirley Holland said. "All this is my problem, and none of yours."

On the television screen here was the dim luminous blue of early morning, and snow on low hills patched with evergreen. From far off a dark figure proceeded toward the camera, then the picture cut and the figure was closer, then a series of quick cuts until the man on snowshoes was close enough to recognize. It was the dead man, the man Shirley Holland recognized as Danzig. Another thing to try and make sense of. Shirley Holland shut off the television while Danzig grinned into the camera and pulled off his stocking cap. The same sort of cap the kid had been wearing. Maybe they all wore caps. Holland touched the granular sandstone mantel above the ash-filled fireplace. Some one of these children had scrubbed the years of soot form the yellow stone that was rough as sandpaper under his fingertips, but his initials were still there, S H inside a heart, alongside the names and initials of the men who had been his friends in those days.

Now that he was able to look at them, there were five of them dead in this big room. It was hard to tell which were the boys and which were girls, what with their long hair and the same kind of clothes, work shirts and raggedy Levi's and wool socks, no shoes or boots on any of them, five dead children on that hardwood floor. Five was the right number. There was Danzig dead in the pickup, and there was the kid in town with Doris. That added up to seven. Seven backpacks and seven sets of binoculars and seven automatic rifles and the sign on the wall: THE SEVEN DWARFS. That made it perfect.

They must have sanded and varnished the floor because it shone like it never had in the old days. The green wall was tattooed with bullet holes in two long undulating rows, holes that could only have been made by one of the automatic rifles leaning against the green wall by the backpacks. The weapons were Swedish BAR, M-37, and loaded. Shirley Holland lifted one and was surprised at how heavy it was in his hands. As he held the automatic rifle he imagined old television pictures of vague jungles in Vietnam, and they changed with the weight of that rifle in his hands; he could nearly taste the sour green of the swampy tropics as he held the rifle waist high and turned, imagining the heavy racketing sound the rifle would make, the bullets fluttering around the room. If he went outside and fired a couple of rounds into the propane tank the place would burn. "Billy," he called, and when he looked out the open door there was Billy with flakes of snow melting on his plaid jacket, still holding the .38 Detective Special.

"Billy," Holland said, "you put the safety on, and put that damned thing away. Make yourself a snowball or something. There is not going to be anybody here."

Then Holland turned away and did it, he touched the trigger and the rifle jumped in his hands, stronger and more forceful than he had imagined, the sound louder, battering and harsh inside that room, quicker than he had thought; and there was another short row of holes in the green wall, Holland thought, *Billy, there's Billy out on the porch*, and he spun, ready to fall and roll if Billy should come in shooting and crazy, but only ended up standing there with the automatic rifle aimed at the open doorway.

Heading for the pickup, he thought, and he imagined Billy running down through the snow, toward the bridge. Should have got his keys away from him. "Billy," Holland said, "you all right?"

"Yeah." Billy stepped through the doorway. He was smiling, and the .38 was in his shoulder holster.

"What we're going to do," Shirley Holland said, surprised by the idea as he said it, "is stay the night, and see what is what around here." He waited for the insolence to slip out of Billy's eyes.

"There is food on the stove," Billy said. "They were cooking. Someone shut off the burners." Billy was shaking a pair of silver-mounted spurs with rowels big as cartwheel dollars, and the clinking sound was like someone slowly walking. "These spurs," Billy said, as if there was nothing to fear, "were on a nail out there. Whoever it was had to be horseback. There's no tracks otherwise."

Billy clinked the spurs again, his eyes almost vacantly intent, like the business of this night had seared over the soft place in his head that made him always afraid. Holland knew what it was, the overload from seeing too many bodies. Enough of that and the dead become different from you, no more important than broken chairs.

"Billy," Shirley Holland said, "we better have a drink. We better warm up some of that stew and have a drink. What you do, you warm up whatever they were eating and I'll walk down to the pickup and get the bottle." His hands were shaking, and Holland knew he was not going to stay the night. What a crazy idea! The idea was to have some hot food and a drink, and then leave. When he was outside, halfway down the lane toward the bridge, Holland realized he was still carrying the automatic rifle, and he laid it carefully in the snow, walked a few more feet, then went back and carried the rifle down to the bridge and dropped it off into the darkness where the small stream had cut away the drifted snow.

The stew was thick with chopped leeks. The girl dead on the floor just beyond the stove must have been a vegetarian, they must have all been vegetarians, because the only meat in the stew was bits of fish and shrimp and clams. With his belly filled, Shirley Holland was finally looking closely at one of the dead, the girl sprawled on the floor beyond the stove, near the long laboratory table where the elaborate Bausch & Lomb microscope, fitted out with camera attachments, sat like a huge gray metal mantis hibernating toward spring. Between the stove and the microscope a worn oriental rug hung like a tapestry from the ceiling, forming a room divider. The side nearest the stove was slick with grease. It was then, touching the rug, his belly warm with stew and whiskey hot in his throat, that Shirley Holland thought about vegetarians and knew he was wrong. Somebody had been frying meat.

The girl, when he brushed her long reddish hair back off her face, this one was clearly a girl, heavy breasted in a white embroidered peasant's blouse, this girl's face was thin and almost foreign looking. Even with that nose she must have been close to beautiful before she fell and bit halfway through her tongue.

"Maybe it's important," Holland said.

"What?" Billy Kumar was still carrying his spoon.

"That they turned off the stove." Whoever walked out of this alive had cared enough and been sensible enough to shut off the burners, which in turn meant not crazy. Or maybe it meant crazy enough, or else it meant nothing. Most likely it meant whoever it was had been used to taking care of things in this house. Which meant nothing again, because he knew the kid had been here. So maybe the kid had turned off the burners, even with his sister dead. Which one was the sister? Surely not this one, she couldn't be the sister, not with that nose.

"So maybe it's the kid," Billy Kumar said, "back there with Doris."

"Don't pay no attention about Doris," Shirley Holland said.

"That's Doris all right," Billy Kumar said.

"How's that?"

"Doris can do all right."

Shirley Holland grunted and turned on the light in the microscope and peered down through the eyepiece. The instrument was focused on what looked like a hair, thick and cellular in magnification against a glaring white background. Holland shut off the light. Looking through a thing like that was like driving through snow, it got you to seeing the wrong sides of complications where there was only this simple problem: what happened? And that was equally simple. Someone had sprayed these people with M-37 bullets, and the blood that had splattered everywhere in this room, the bullet holes in the green wall, that was what had been going on in here. It was time to go home. They ought to stop touching and moving things and send some fingerprint people to figure things out until the dark touch of a killer came clear.

"What I am going to do," Holland said, " is leave you here to stand guard. I am going back to town and let you look after things here for the night. Maybe whoever it is will come back, and you can get him."

Billy Kumar smiled like that was a good idea. "All right," Billy said, "you do that."

"Not really," Holland said. "Let's shut off the stove and close the door on this place."

"I mean it," Billy said. "It don't bother me a bit."

"It ought to," Holland said.

"Just so long as you see I ain't chickenshit," Billy said. "There's no way I am chickenshitting out on this. Just so you know that."

"I got that straight," Holland said. "You are not chickenshit. You are a hard man to frighten."

"That's good," Billy said. "There is nothing to worry about out here. He's back in town with Doris. Back there is where you got to start worrying."

It wasn't until then, watching Billy shut off the burners on the stove, the dying blue flicker of propane, that Holland knew which one was the sister. She was the one slumped at the foot of the stairway leading up to the second floor and the bedrooms. This was in some way her fault. Holland could see it, the kid standing near the doorway with the automatic rifle, the sister coming arrogantly down the stairs after the kid called her, his voice shrill and angry, some disdainful remark from the sister, dismissing his anger, and this touch of the finger, the hammering sound as the bullets traced their way back and forth across that green wall, and all of them dead. A quarrel from childhood finally resolved. But maybe it wasn't that way. Maybe Danzig had gone first, shot down off that D7 in the late afternoon, as the kid rode in; maybe all this was planned.

There was no telling, but for sure no one but the kid could have stood there with the M-37 while they all went on about the business of their cooking. Only the kid could have swept the room with that M-37 like he was blowing it clean with a hose.

The girl at the bottom of the stairs had a plain country face and short dark hair, and Holland knew he was right. She was the sister. Holland stepped over her and climbed the stairs toward the darkness up there, and when he switched on the light in the room directly across from the head of the stairway, he knew he was even more right. It was a bedroom, there was no door, not even a curtain hanging in the doorway, no privacy, but it was a room where people slept. There was a double-bed mattress on the floor, covered with a fake-looking oriental rug that had been spattered with yellow paint, and a long table and a chair under the dark window in the far wall, but furnishings were not what was important.

What mattered was the dead man. A small dark man, maybe a Puerto Rican or a Cuban or Malaysian, one of the fine-boned dark people from some other continent; he was curled in the far corner of the room, and had been chopped apart with short crossing sweeps of the M-37, literally cut up in the work of the night. His face was torn apart, and his intestines spilled and burst, blood and greenish fecal matter pooled together and drying on the flooring. The man had been naked except for a pair of avocado green nylon bikini shorts. You poor lonesome little bastard, Holland thought, he got you fine, didn't he. Which will teach you to trust in white girls.

So this is the reason, Holland thought, the old reasons. Posters on the wall, and snowmobiles down in the barn where the teams of work-mares once steamed on winter mornings while they snuffled at their oats, automatic rifles and whatever these kids thought they were going to force toward perfection, and now there is this same old trouble. Danzig first; Danzig was older, and had money, and was just playing. Holland didn't blame the kid for getting Danzig first, making sure of that much.

The soap bear: the tiny precisely carved fangs.

The soap bear sat surrounded by whittled shards of the hard yellow laundry soap it had come from, alone on the table under the window except for the elaborately compartmented hardwood box of thin-bladed Exacto carving knives, chisels and tiny chrome-plated hammers, needles that might be used for etching. The girl had been starting herself a career in carving. Winter could lock you into seeing how you could be somebody else while you watched out a second-story window to where snowbirds were playing. Holland tested the blade of one of the

Exacto knives against the back of his thumbnail. It was as factory sharp as any knife he had ever honed. Once in the lobby of the U.S. National Bank in Cody, Wyoming, waiting for a check to go through, Holland watched a man carve the head of an eagle from dark hardwood. That man had been using tools exactly like these. They looked like instruments that might belong to a dentist.

And how sure-handed she had been. Holland wondered if she had been at her carving just before she was called down the stairs to die. Holland could see it, the little dark man sleeping in his avocado green undershorts, and the girl at her work, the call from downstairs, whatever tool she had been using placed neatly back into the compartmented box; and then the racketing of the automatic rifle when she reached the bottom of the stairway. Holland imagined the little dark man terrified and confused from his sleep as the killer came slowly up after him, the dark man cringing in the corner, and the unforgiving stare of the gunman. Not even then will you believe it, Holland thought, not until you are dead will you know it has happened.

Holland picked up the soap bear. The body was only roughed in behind the shoulders, but the head was carved in great detail, the ears, the fangs, and the ruffled hump of a grizzly by someone who knew what she was doing. It was nice work. Those years ago they carved their names roughly in the sandstone mantel over the fireplace, and that roughness had worked out better than this fine touch. But maybe not: there was always the scorching odor of piss in that memory. Holland shook his head and went down the stairs, left the lights burning and headed out into the snow. "Which one," Billy said, "do you figure was the sister?"

"I figure they all was," Holland said, waiting on the porch, "I figure they was all his sister. We might as well get down the road."

"Not me," Billy said. "I'm staying here."

"You ain't hired to do what you want," Holland said.

"Fine," Billy said. "Then I quit. I'm staying here."

"I guess you are," Holland said. "You stay here. Never mind the quitting. You stay here and guard the evidence." Holland slipped the soap bear under his coat, where it would be out of the snow. The moisture might melt one of those fine touches. You stay here, he thought, and then you can figure on twenty years of not being upset by anything because you've seen it all now. It will do you good to stay.

When he reached the pickup, Holland shone his flashlight into Danzig's iced-over face. He brushed the snow away. Private television, he thought. You must have been one fancy asshole to gather all this trouble into one household. Billy had followed him down from the house. "There ain't no good in it," Billy said, "in staying here. In town is where the killer is."

3

Frilled and embroidered, the nylon robe swept the carpet silently as Doris Holland came barefoot into the living room. Sitting herself on the floor before the fireplace, she drew open the brass fire doors. Opening the leather-bound picture album, she quickly snapped three of the photographs from the holders fastening them to the page. She flicked each photo into the cold fireplace with a quick motion of her wrist. Then she reached in, and drew out the little pile of photographs, as if she must begin again, properly.

After switching on the small cut-glass chandelier in the

room she took up the pictures again, this time examining each before dropping it into the fireplace. Occasionally, she would come across old photographs of Holland, a long-haired ragged boy squinting into the sun from the bed of a Ford V-8 truck, crouching with baby geese beside spring tules, pictures of old people she had never known, gone or dead before she ever saw Holland, a gray-haired woman, wearing a sagging flowered dress and a gambling-man sun visor, standing beside an ancient black automobile and scowling. These photos she set aside, intending them for Holland. Only when the pile for burning was bigger than she had imagined it could be—she never remembered posing for so many pictures—as she was heading down the hallway toward the kitchen for matches, did she think of how the fire would look, flame, and then a curling mound of cellulose that would resemble the final moments of a doll burning, the yellow feathery hair and the little clothes gone, the plastic body curling into the insides of itself. She pulled a hair from her head and struck a match and lighted the hair and watched it burn before she left the pictures piled there in the firebox and went back up the stairs to where the boy was sleeping. So many pictures of herself; Doris in a yellow dress, down by the river on a Sunday, her face soft and drunk and her bright lipstick in that fuzzy old-time World War II color, smeary red. She couldn't bring herself to start the fire.

"They go strange on you," Holland said. "It's not like they are stupid. It's just that they never had any chances to learn anything." The night was turning gray toward daylight, and they were driving slowly along the muffled side streets, only a couple of blocks from his house and the jailhouse across the way. "What you have to remember," Holland said, "with people who have gone crazy or wherever they have gone, is that they are like animals. There is nothing like a human being in there."

At least the snow had stopped. His gray two-story house with the towering Colorado blue spruce in front looked like no one had ever come or gone from it this night. The heavy snowfall had buried even his own tracks. All the windows were dark, there was that to think about. Doris always left a light on in the living room. An untouched world in the morning. Holland parked in the driveway and reached over and slapped Billy on the knee. "We are going to tell them stories," he said, "when this mud is settled."

Up there at the Frantz place he had carved his name over the mantel. "Funny how you would never do that in your own house," Holland said. Billy didn't answer. Holland tried to think of something in this house, his house, where he had lived since the year he was eleven, something that would seem as real to his memory as touching that sandstone and carving those initials. He shut off the idling pickup. How do you go to your own house when something has gone bad on the inside, when it doesn't seem like your place to live anymore, when you almost cannot recall living there although it was the place where you mostly ate and slept for all of your grown-up life? Try to remember cooking one meal.

"There is no use stalling on it," Billy said. "This time I am taking the shotgun. We got to go in there after him."

"You take the front," Billy said. "They won't suspect you. I'll cover the back. You give me a key to the back door, and I'll come around on them."

"What?"

"I'll cover the back."

"You just sit quiet," Holland said. "You leave that shotgun where it is, and you sit here quiet. There is nothing

wrong in there, and if there is, I am not having you and
that shotgun in my house."

"Is that an order?"

"Yes," Holland said, "that is an order. You will sit here
quiet and I will go inside and turn on the lights, and then
I will wave to you from the door, and you will not bring
the shotgun. That is an order."

So there it was. Doris and that kid, side by side and sleeping, like no one would ever come up the creaking stairs a
step at a time with a pistol drawn, to shoot them in that
bed where he had always slept until now. Sometimes
there is no choice but to walk into your own house. Far
away, you think, and you do not want to see. You come
home and you say do not tell me. You say, I have hunted
the elk all over the snowfields of the Selway, and I do not
want to know what happened here. And then there is a
morning you walk in and take a look in your own house,
like any traveler.

The .38 Detective Special was cold as a rock in his
hand, and Holland thought: I could kill them, one and
two and done with, except for being an old man alone
down there in that living room, and the explanations.

"Are they there?" It was Billy, whispering loud from
the bottom of the stairway. Billy with his own .38 Detective Special in his hand. You could walk away, down the
stairs, and tell Billy no. You could tell Billy no and go
across to the jail and start making telephone calls, to the
coroner and the state police, and come back here later,
and say you don't know how you missed them, you don't
understand how they could have been here all the time
in your own house, and overlooked.

"Yeah," Holland said, and his voice was loud and harsh.
"Yeah, they are sure as hell here. You ought to see them

here. You come on up and see them." Holland switched on the bedroom lights as they came fighting awake under the bedclothes to see him standing with that black pistol in his hand, the bearded kid and Doris, her face soft and old without the eyeglasses, Doris sitting up and her breasts flat and naked, hanging and empty in the way she never let him see. Holland just stood there, giving them some time to figure out who they were going to be this morning.

"If this ain't hell," Holland said, when Doris just went on sitting there uncovered, her eyes out of focus without the eyeglasses. "I always figured it would be me," Holland said. "Some one of these whiskey tramps would come in and find me shacking down with his lady, and I would be sitting there wondering if he would shoot, and when." He could hear Billy coming up the stairs, one step at a time.

"Billy," Holland said, "forget it. Go on back down. We will all be down in a minute. I'm coming down." Holland turned back to the bed.

"The two of you get dressed," Holland said, "and then you come down the stairs and we will have some coffee and talk about what is going to happen next." Holland went over and shook the kid's clothing to make sure there was no gun, and then he left them.

But that was a mistake. At the bottom of the stairs he knew it was a mistake. Racked in the corner of his closet there was the 30-30 his father had left, and the scope-sighted 30-06 Holland carried while hunting mule deer and elk, and the two shotguns, the 12-gauge for Canada geese and mallards, and the 20-gauge for brush birds, pheasant and quail and the chuckers he had one time hunted down on the far desert rimrock country of south-eastern Oregon, near the Nevada border on the bare sage-brush mountains. And there were stacks of boxed shells alongside the weapons.

With Billy hovering behind him while he made coffee in the kitchen, Holland knew he had made the bad mistake and tried to think about something else. There was no use going back up the stairs, either the kid had one of the shotguns or he didn't. And sure enough, he did. When Holland turned from plugging in the coffee, the kid was standing there in the doorway to the kitchen, barefoot and naked except for his pants, holding the 12-gauge. Doris stood behind him, wrapped in a blanket. Billy had turned useless again, standing by the electric stove with his arms reaching upward, pointing the .38 at the ceiling. Holland raised his own hands. "You stay calm," Holland said, "and we will give up our weapons, and we will all have us a cup of coffee with sugar and cream to get us warm."

"Billy," Holland said, "bring the weapon down very slowly, aiming it toward the window, and drop it in the sink."

"And Doris," Holland said, "you come over here and you pick my weapon out of my holster, and you take both mine and Billy's and you throw them out the back door into the snow. Then we will be all right, and we will have some coffee."

Except for the gun, it was like a holiday, or one of those Sundays after a winter dance with people sleeping over, when everyone wakes up half drunk and that is fine because there is nothing to do but sit around the kitchen and sip coffee with no thought that Monday is coming. Four cups of steaming coffee and the gray morning light through the windows, and only the kid tipped back in his chair with one of the .38 Detective Special pistols in his hand to mar the scene. "If you won't shoot," Holland said, "I would get a shot of whiskey from under the sink. There is another bottle under there."

"The whiskey is in the living room," Doris said, "on the mantel. We had some last night. He was shaking and dying."

"Well then, you get the bottle for me," Holland said. "Please, or he will shoot me if I try to get it for myself."

"What you might think," Doris said, "is not true. He needed body warmth. He was dying of cold. You can understand that."

"I understand that," Holland said. "Body warmth and dying of cold. Why don't you get me the whiskey, and we will all feel better in a little while."

"No," the kid said, when Doris had gone for the whiskey, "we won't feel any better. My sister is dead, you saw them, they are all dead up there, and no whiskey is going to make us feel any better."

"We could have some whiskey in our coffee anyway," Holland said. "We have all been out in the cold, and the whiskey can't hurt."

"That's right," the kid said, and for the first time his eyes did not slide away from Holland's. "We all been out in the cold. There's a way you get sick when you been too long out in the cold, not so much freezing or anything as just shivering and you can't think. The part to notice first is that you can't think right. There is a name for it, Danzig knew the name, and you can die from it. Last night when I came in here I couldn't think right, and she took care of me. That's all there was. The cure is dry clothing and body warmth. There is a name for it."

"That woman," Holland said. "I don't know what she made of you but you got to understand she is an old woman. Just yesterday she was not an old woman, but now she is. There is all kinds of ways to go sick. Just thinking about all those dead people can make you go strange."

"Danzig knew the name for it," the kid said.

"Danzig taught you plenty, didn't he?" Holland said.

"There was one thing that was good about Danzig," the kid said, tipping his chair forward, sitting with his elbows on his knees, the .38 Detective Special aimed at Holland as Doris came back with the whiskey bottle, "and that was that he knew things."

"Go ahead," the kid said, motioning at the whiskey bottle with the pistol, "go ahead and pour. Some whiskey would be all right for you. You been out like I was. But you got to understand there was something wrong with Danzig. He wanted the right things, but there was something wrong.

"When I was growing up," the kid said, "you knew my father. His name was Mac Banta, and he lived down there in the Bitterroot."

"I never knew anybody named Banta," Holland said.

"Well, he was there anyway," the kid said, "and there was those spring mornings with the geese flying north, and I would stand out on the lawn with the sun just coming up and the fence painted white around my mother's roses, and it would be what my father called a bluebird morning. That is what Danzig wanted, bluebird mornings. My sister would be there, and my mother and my father, and the birds playing in the lilac. Comes down to a world of hurt was what my father would say, and he would laugh because nothing could hurt you on those bluebird mornings. And that is what Danzig wanted."

Holland poured the whiskey and sat there in his kitchen, the four of them around the oak kitchen table while the kid talked and fondled the .38, all of them but the kid sipping at the coffee and whiskey and listening while the kid told them about Danzig, and Danzig's money, and the way Danzig was going to stop everything with those automatic rifles and snowmobiles and the closed-circuit television, seeing there was no need for anything but bluebird mornings. "But he lost interest," the kid said, "and after a while it was like he was just playing. After a while all any of them were doing up there was just smoking dope and fucking."

The kid named Banta turned to look at Doris. "I am sorry for saying that," he said, "but that is all any of them were doing up there, smoking dope and fucking. There is no other way to say it. That is when I left. My sister, Grace, she wouldn't go, she was worse than any of them, so I left her there.

"And now she is dead," Banta said, "and she cried. I could see the tears on her face. But it was Danzig who should have cried."

"Boy," Holland said, "let me show you something. Out there on the seat of my pickup there is a carving. You let me show you that carving. You let Doris go out and get me that carving, and I will show you something."

They stood by the picture window in the living room and watched Doris go out barefoot in the snow and open the pickup with her blanket wrapped around her like some native woman and come back with the soap bear. In the kitchen they sat back around the oak table while the kid stared at the face of the carving, the intricate fangs of the soap bear, and the fine etched ruff of hair over the hump. "Now let me show you something," Holland said, and he took the carving from the boy and carried it to the sink. Holland turned on the hot water, and let it go until it was steaming, and held the head of the bear under the flow, and then with his hands burning he began to rub and wash at the slippery foaming soap until the tiny etched lines were gone and the carving was mostly gone, until there was nothing but the smooth wet surface of what had been as precise and as perfect as that girl could make it be. Holland held the dripping object out toward the boy. "Now you look at this," Holland said. "You have come in here and you have ruined some things of mine, and now I have ruined what your sister was doing that you did not know a thing about. Every mark your sister made is slicked away. So you lift up your head and shoot me if you think you can, but there is one thing about it, and that is that we are even right now. You have done me some damage, coming into my house like you have, and I have done you some damage, but maybe you have the best of it because some morning you might come to see that nobody ever did owe you any bluebirds, not ever. But maybe that same morning you might see that the best bluebird you ever had was that soap bear, and it washed away so easy. So we are even. You shoot me if you got the notion, but I am willing to call it even.

"Or what you could do," Holland said, "is get up and walk out of this kitchen and out of here. There is a chance you could go upstairs and get into your clothes while we all sit around this table, and you could leave. If you are smart at all, that is what you will do. If you didn't leave any absolutely fresh prints up with those dead people nobody will ever be able to pin you with all that mess, and you will get away free. If you shoot me you will have to shoot everyone here, and you are a dead man then. You have wiped your sister clean, and you have got Danzig clean, but there is no way you can get everything to stay clean. Maybe you ought to just leave things go the way they are for a while, and walk out. People like you," Holland said, "are always forgetting the ghosts there are in this world."

"There is too much," the kid said, "you don't forget. You start letting those things go and you are not anybody. You got it painted on the outside of your jailhouse. When I was a kid in high school we laughed about that, and Danzig, he laughed about that. A new world every morning. Wake up and nothing counts from yesterday.

"And you know what?" the kid said, "That is bullshit. You know what they were doing up there? You know what my sister did for Christmas? She cooked three turkeys. And you know what she did? She painted them all green with food coloring. Did you ever think about eating a green turkey? Did you ever see green stuffing? Green birds for a green world was what she said, like turkeys should be the color of grass. Springtime turkeys is what she called them. That is what you end up with. A new world every morning, and you got green turkeys." The kid went on tapping the table with the pistol barrel, leaving tiny marks in the polished hardwood surface.

"It was a joke," Holland said. "The sign was a joke."

"Well, the fun is over," the kid said.

"Not just yet." It was Billy Kumar, and he held a palm-sized one-shot gambler's gun of the kind Holland had seen only in Western movies. From somewhere in his clothing, while the kid preached at Holland, Billy had come out with that tiny weapon, with a chrome-plated barrel only about an inch and a half long, and he held it aimed straight at the side of the kid's head, dead on Virgil Banta from three or four feet. All this time, Holland thought, he had been packing that thing hidden.

"We got one more piece of fun," Billy Kumar said, and even though his hand was trembling just so slightly, Billy didn't look frightened, not even angry, but more like a great door had just swung wide and he was seeing the first thing he ever liked in his life, his eyes squinted and lips pulled back, and chewing at just the tip of his tongue. "You drop that pistol. Just open your hand and let it drop."

"Billy," Holland said. "Wait a minute."

"I am going to kill the old man," Virgil Banta said, not moving. "On the count of three I am going to kill the old man."

Billy almost missed. His one shot struck Virgil Banta in the shoulder, but that was enough. The kid didn't even fire. Maybe that is to his credit, Holland thought later, maybe he didn't mean to fire. But at the time, as Holland rolled sideways out of his chair, knowing there would be a second explosion of fire in the room, directly in his face, the shot that never came, he was thinking he had killed himself. All my life, he was thinking, knowing Billy was beyond his control even before the shot. All my life, Holland was thinking, waiting for this, some cockeyed son of a bitch getting me killed. All my life getting myself killed.

"He thought you would understand," Doris said, "that was why he came here, thinking you would understand."

"What am I to understand?" Holland said. "He is up there in my bedroom jackass naked, along with you, and I am supposed to make something wonderful out of that? He was a murderer, and he was crazy.

"But then forget it," Holland said. "Which is what I mean—forget it. This is all something to forget."

It was late darkening afternoon; and the blood had been scrubbed from the kitchen floor; and the Banta kid was safe in the county hospital with federal deputies guarding him; and Billy Kumar was gone home with his pearl-handled one-shot Las Vegas gambler gun, gone home to be a new man; and Shirley Holland was at his kitchen table again, picking at a bacon-and-mushroom omelet. Thick country bacon, and none of those canned mushrooms, the real mushrooms Doris gathered down on the sandy riverbanks of the Clark Fork in spring just as the cottonwoods were coming into fresh leaf. Real mushrooms frozen for winter. One cup of coffee, Holland thought, and then I will go to sleep. Outside the window over the sink, snow was falling thick again. "What could I have understood?" Holland said, and he wondered what those children thought as they scrubbed the soot off a sandstone mantelpiece where someone had carved a heart with the letters S H inside. What did they understand?

"Nothing," Doris said, "It's just what he thought, he thought you would understand. Nothing happened up there. I swear. Holland?"

"Fine," Holland said. "The first good spring day, a warm day, I am going to paint out that sign. You get to be my age, and a thing like that isn't anything you want to think about seriously."

Doris didn't even look around from where she was rinsing the frying pan.

"Nothing happened," Doris said.

"It never does."

This time it was a girl Halverson knew, halfway eaten and her hair chewed off. She had been awake in the night; she'd been afraid and whimpering as the great bear nudged at the side of the nylon tent like a rooting hog. She held to the other girl's hand, and began to scream only when the long claws ripped her out of her sleeping bag, continuing to scream as she was being dragged away, the feather down from the sleeping bag floating above the glowing coals of a pine-knot fire. This time it was someone he knew; and he lay still in the darkness and the warmth of his own bed and tried to understand the feeling of knowing you were killed before you were dead.

Thinking was beyond the point. The last time Halverson lay awake like this, the first weekend the hard wind-drifted snow was plowed off the Going-to-the-Sun Highway over Logan Pass, it had been a fetus—not a fetus really, a child, stillborn, a baby girl dropped in a roadside trash container at the east end of Two Medicine Lake and found by workmen. A dead baby wrapped in a pink motel towel and thrown into a garbage can. It could not have been anything like indifference that brought someone to such a burial. More like the need to get rid of what can happen. Walk into the wind and your eyes will water.

But in the beginning there was Darby, and the way Halverson saw her avoiding mirrors. There was no explaining

it to Darby, but early in May, when the aspen leaves along
the middle fork of the Flathead were lime green and just
emerging, Halverson began to think he saw what Darby
was seeing when she quickly looked away from the long
mirror she'd hung in his bedroom. Halverson would
glance up on the evenings when she was home and see
Darby with her stockinged feet up on the hearth before
the fire, intent on one of her magazines—the old issues of
the *National Geographic* she brought with her when she
came to live with him—and he would see her as she would
look when she was old. Her eyeglasses would be thicker
and distorting her eyes until they were strange as the eyes
of owls; eventually, he knew, she would be fumbling and
blind. Her hands would touch at things she could not see,
tentative and exploring. If he stayed with her long enough
there would be the time when she fell, the cracking of
bone, a sound he imagined as he watched her turn the
magazine pages; and some indeterminate time after that,
he would be alone and old, his hands touching and exploring each thing in this familiar room as he talked to some
memory of his father about sharpening a knife or the color
of hatchery trout.

Halverson told Darby that he would never have children if he had anything to say about it. He told her that
he could not go on living with her, and that he would not
ever try living with another woman. He told her they
were better off alone.

"I'm sorry," he told her, expecting her to argue. But
she only looked back to her magazine.

"No," she said. "It's not that."

The next night, when he came home from hauling
cedar logs, his cabin was filled with chairs and tables
made of twisted and shellacked bamboo. Bright patterns
of lavender and orange tropical flowers were splashed

across the cushions. His old furniture was piled out in the pole barn where he sheltered the truck in winter. "Don't you think about worrying," Darby said. "This is all in my name. I'm making the payments. Fifty-seven dollars a month." There was a new canvas drop cloth over the chair on his side of the fireplace, so the fabric would stay clean.

"While I pay for every bite there is to eat," Halverson said. There had been nothing kind he could say.

"I always wanted this," Darby said. "It's like the South Pacific, don't you think?"

"Pretty close," Halverson said. He didn't mention the notion of her leaving again.

That which is not useful is vicious: in needlepoint, those words had been framed on his grandfather's wall, attributed to Cotton Mather. Halverson's father burned the plaque along with the bedding heaped on the bed where his grandfather had shivered away his last months. The blankets smelled of camphor as they burned. Halverson's grandfather had died angry, refusing to eat and starving himself. His father had never helped his mother try to make the old man eat, but had sat in the kitchen glaring at the snowfall outside the window over the sink while the persuading went on. Halverson had been six or seven, but he could still hear his mother's voice murmuring from the old man's room at the back of the house.

"There is only so much sin for each of us," his mother had repeated over and over. Halverson had never thought of it much until now, but he knew the old man had not been sinning.

In the bedroom, the digital clock atop Halverson's Sony TV showed the time to be 12:52. The pint of Jack Daniel's was empty and Halverson was nowhere near sleep. He always tried to be sleeping when Darby came home late from her bartending shift. He didn't want to hear who had gone off with the wrong partner at closing time, or which children slept in the car while their parents drank and quarreled after the drive-in movie.

But tonight there was the girl; she was young, and now she was dead, the round slope of her tight belly eaten away by the grizzly. Her hair, which hung down her back in a tangled red-tinted rope, had been gnawed off her skull. Park rangers were searching with rifles. Halverson got up and went into the bathroom and turned the shower to steaming hot, then down to cold while he stood under the spray, trying not to gasp or flinch. He shaved for the second time that day, and then pulled a flannel shirt from his closet, turned the cuffs up, and dragged on his work pants and laced his boots. His face was smooth and slick as he rubbed at his eyes, thinking: just this one time, just tonight, another drink.

The girl who died had worked in the bar where Darby worked. Halverson stopped there each evening for his pint of Jack Daniel's and a glass or two of beer. He'd joked with the girl only a few nights ago about how she was going to be stuck in this country if she stayed much longer. "Five years . . . you can't help going native." It had been something to say while she rang up the pint. She was a dark and not exceptionally pretty girl who had come west from a rich suburb of Columbus, Ohio. She had quit the Wildlife Biology School down in Missoula and come to Columbia Falls with a boy who sold cocaine to the skiers in Whitefish and spent his summers climbing mountains. Halverson wondered what happened to you with cocaine. When the boy was caught and sentenced to five years in the state prison at Deer Lodge, maybe three years with probation, she took the barmaid job and said she was going to wait. According to Darby, she had been; there hadn't been any fooling around.

Halverson drove down the canyon from his cabin toward the neon thickness of light over Columbia Falls. Outside the tavern he parked and listened to the soft racketing of the tappets in his Land Rover.

Halverson sat watching the beer signs flicker on and off, and then he drove home. Below the cabin, he parked the Land Rover beside the shadowy bulk of his 350 Kenworth diesel log-hauling truck. Halverson spent his working days drifting the truck down the narrow asphalt alongside the Flathead River, hauling cedar logs to the shake mill below Hungry Horse. The amber-hearted cedar smelled like medicine ought to smell. The work was like a privilege, mostly asphalt under the tires and those logs. And now he was quitting.

Halverson climbed up and sat in the Kenworth, snapped on the headlights so they shone into the scrub brush at the edge of the timber. He was not going out the next morning. The truck was ready, log bunks chained down for the trip into the mountains before sunrise, but he was not going to work come morning.

He was imagining the bear. The dished face of the great animal would rear up simple and inquisitive from vines where serviceberries hung thick as wine grapes. The dark nose would be a target under the crosshairs. The sound of the shot would reverberate between the mineral-striped walls of the cirque, where the glaciers had spent their centuries eating away rock. Far away a stone would be dislodged and come rattling down over the slide. The square-headed peaks would dampen the sound to silence.

Halverson could hear the stone clattering on other stones after the echo of the shot diminished to nothing.

But he could not imagine the animal falling. He couldn't imagine anything beyond that first shot. Halverson shut off the headlights on the Kenworth and went into the cabin and punched off the alarm, and was satisfied to sleep.

The girl had died two nights ago in the backcountry of Glacier Park. With another girl, she'd camped at the distant eastern end of Quartz Lake in the Livingston Range. Here there were no trails cut through the deadfall lodgepole along the shore, the section of the park kept closest to true wilderness, miles from other campers. It was territory Halverson knew, from those late-summer encampments his father had called vacations. All his working life Halverson's father had drawn wages from the park: trail-crew supervisor in the summer and snow clearance in the winter; feeding baled hay to the elk and deer during the really bad winters. Each September after the Labor Day tourists had gone home, his father took time to camp in the backcountry, to hide out, as he said, and let his whiskers grow and learn to smell himself again. You go and forget who you are, his father said, when you never get wind of yourself. The time that don't count, his father liked to say, meaning a thing John Muir said about wandering in the mountains: *the time that will not bo subtracted from the sum of your life.* But something had been subtracted. His father died of a heart seizure, defibrillation the doctors called it, when he was thirty-nine years old. There was a winter morning when Halverson's mother stood in the lighted bedroom doorway, saying to Halverson, "Don't you come in here!" Then there was the door closing, and her shrieking. *You don't come in here!* After a while she was quiet. And then she came out of the bedroom and closed the door and washed her face. Then she turned to Halverson and said, *he is dead.*

Halverson was now forty-two, three years older than his father had been when he died. He had not been in the park, except to shortcut through, since his father's funeral. What year could that have been?

The girl who survived told of awakening to hear the bear grunting outside the tent, and the other girl whimpering. What I thought, the girl said, is *thank God it is out there*. That was all I could think, like I knew there was a bear outside, but it was *outside*, you see. The girl who survived told how she and the other girl held hands and tried to stay quiet. Then the nylon tent ripped away, and the vast dark animal dragging the other girl from her sleeping bag; and the beginning of the screaming, really just long breathless shrieking as the bear killed her. That was the way she told it, the girl who survived; *he just dragged her away and killed her.* After a while, the girl said, I climbed a tree. The insides of her thighs were torn by the bark. But it didn't make any difference, the girl said, he didn't come for me, he didn't want me.

The girl spent most of the next day making her way out along the six-mile rocky shoreline of Quartz Lake, back toward the trails and other hikers. Before nightfall the hunt began. Rangers with rifles dropped at the shore of the lake from helicopters and discovered the half-eaten body. Halverson burned the newspaper in his fireplace, and looked around at Darby's flowered furniture, remembering her notion of making a getaway to some Pacific island. "Marlon Brando did it," Darby said.

"Three or four days," Halverson told Darby. "You do some bowling or something." He didn't tell her he was heading out of Montana, over to Spokane where nobody would know him, to buy a rifle.

"Which one is it?"

"Nobody," he said. "I wouldn't be chasing a woman."

Halverson spent two days talking to gun men in the surplus houses and sporting-goods stores and ended up spending $440 for a falling block Ruger #1, fitted out with a Redfield 3 x 9 variable wide-angle scope and firing a .458 Winchester magnum bullet. One reasonably placed shot would kill anything native to North America, really anything anywhere, the salesman said, except for maybe a whale. Except for maybe a blue whale, and there were not many of them left. The salesman laughed, but then shook his head like there was nothing funny about dead whales.

The walnut stock swung hard and secure against Halverson's shoulder, and the mechanism worked with heavy, poised delicacy. The series of simple firing motions could be performed in two or three seconds, which was important, because the grizzly is as fast as a thoroughbred horse: three hundred yards in twenty seconds on level ground. But the rifle was extravagantly accurate at distance. Breathe, hold, and fire with the soft draw of the fingertip; and the animal would be dead. There should be no need for speed.

Late the second afternoon, Halverson drove to a gun club north of Spokane, beyond the industrial park around the Kaiser aluminum plant. At the gun club he fired nine rounds at range targets, three more for pleasure. The pattern of the last three rounds, at two hundred yards, was smaller than the spread of his fingers: all into the back of the throat, inside past the carnivorous fangs and into the soft and vulnerable flesh above the dark palate. Halverson could see the leafy boughs with their clusters of red and purple berries whipping after the animal fell, and then quiet in the noontime heat. When he finished firing, his shoulder ached like it had been struck a dozen times with a heavy mallet. The next day he outfitted himself with a light, down-filled sleeping bag and a one-man sleeve tent, a lightweight butane GAZ stove that nested with cooking pots, a spoon and fork and an elaborate Swiss Army knife, and a Buck skinning knife, packets of freeze-dried food in heavy aluminum foil, and detailed hikers' maps of Glacier Park. He knew the park well enough, but the maps, with their shaded precision, were like verification of his accuracy. The bill for the heavy-duty backpack and the traveling gear was almost as much as he'd paid for the rifle, but that was fine with him. Halverson had worked twenty-three years to earn a paid-off Kenworth, and now his time had come and he could just write checks. The gear would start with him, new and clean, and would wear and stain and become his in the wilderness.

Darby was awake. Just out of the shower and blow-drying her hair at the kitchen table while she sipped instant coffee. Halverson had driven back from Spokane in the early morning hours. Now he stood in the doorway with the rifle in his hands. Darby nodded her head, as if acknowledging some premonition. "Who on earth," she said, "can you think you are making plans for?" She was staring at the rifle, the hair-dryer aimed at the ceiling. "Why in the world?" As if this could be his way of making up for her flowered furniture.

So Halverson told her. Just killing one bear, for a head, to mount on the wall, to get things even. Anyway, he said, I never killed one. I am owed one. And no, he told her, she could not come along.

"The rangers killed one," she said. "An old one, a cripple."

Halverson told her it wasn't enough.

"I'm going," Darby said. "I'm going and you can't stop me. I'll just follow."

"Why in the hell?" Halverson said. "This is not any of your concern." No, he told her, she was not going.

"So half the head will be mine," she said.

Halverson mimicked her voice. "What about me?" he said. "How about mine?" He told her she would never make it.

"I got boots," Darby said. "I walk more on a night shift than you walk in three weeks. You better worry about yourself. Back and forth on them duckboards behind that bar is more than you ever think about walking. What you should do is get in some running. Before the moon comes back, you should get in better shape than you are. I can carry extra food, think of that, and you could quit shaving." The hair-dryer looked like a thick-barreled weapon as she shook it while she talked; and the silence after she shut off its whirring let Halverson see how loud their voices had been. There had been the years of climbing through the brush, setting three-quarter-inch cable choker behind the D8 skid Cats when he was breaking in; and then more years bucking a chain saw up those mountains and falling timber, all those years until he had the money for the down payment on the Kenworth, and he was as hard as he would ever need to be. Halverson thought of telling her about how many years he had worked to be in shape for this, but after she shut off the hair-dryer, he didn't say a thing. He kept quiet.

"You come out here." Halverson crossed the kitchen and stood at the open back door, fishing in his coat pocket for a cartridge and then slipping the round into the firing chamber. "You shoot this thing and see. You just see." Darby followed him barefoot out into the weedy lot where he showed her how to hold the rifle, her hands small and white against the stained walnut stock. She almost couldn't reach the trigger.

"Where?"

"Anywhere."

Halverson was surprised by how quick she fired, the roar as she cast a shot toward the timbered hillside. She stepped backward from the recoil. But only for a moment, crouched and regaining her balance, did she look bewildered.

"You should know something," she said. "You are not the first one to try that trick. I been mixed with before by you wise-assed boys." She grinned like a child in the morning sunlight.

"Have it the way you like."

For three weeks, while they waited on the full moon, Halverson kept driving his truck while Darby went on pulling her bartending shift. He gave up on the Jack Daniel's and slept anyway. He lost weight and quit smoking and felt he was becoming less than himself.

They crossed at Polebridge over the North Fork of the Flathead River almost at midnight, under a full moon as they'd planned, carrying enough food for several weeks: the freeze-dried stuff in aluminum packets, a half pound of salt, a brick of cheese; potatoes and onions to fry with the fish he'd catch; and even a heavy uncut side of bacon, Darby's idea. Halverson wanted to travel light. But there was no arguing. "We can camp and you can travel out. We are not going to be moving around. We will make a place." She was carrying her share, and she bought her own gear, every few days bringing home something new to show him: a frameless pack, a Dacron insulated sleeping bag she claimed would dry better than his goose feathers, an expensive breakdown fly rod. She would smile and fondle each thing, as if this was all part of her plan to move away across the Pacific Ocean. As a last gesture, she trimmed his beard. Halverson wanted to shave it off after the first week, because of the itching, and because the gray in it surprised him. "You leave it grow," she told him. "It makes you look like a movie star." After the second week the itching stopped and Halverson got used to it and stopped leaning out to see himself in the huge rectangular mirrors hung on either side of the truck cab. What Darby said was true; he looked like some visitor who might be in town for only a night or so.

The walking was easy in the moonlight, along the twisting roadway past the ranger station at the lower end of Bowman Lake and then on the wide park-service trail over Cerulean Ridge toward Quartz Lake, stepping in and out of the shadows of moonlight. Presently, the early midsummer sun rose in a great blossom over the cirque wall beyond Quartz Lake, near the blunt peak Halverson figured from the map had to be Redhorn, light coming down at them and the shadows receding like tide. Halverson felt as if he could be walking into his childhood where he might find the strange thin-armed boy in his mother's box-camera photographs, himself at thirteen, solemnly holding aloft a small trout; the person he had been, real and turning over stones in a creek, searching for caddis fly larvae, or in a hot meadow catching grasshoppers with his hat. The boy would pay him no attention, intent on catching bait, wearing no shirt under raggedy bib overalls. A boy who existed only in tones of photographic gray.

They got themselves off the trail before there was a chance of meeting other hikers and made a cold camp. As they wove out through the open brush, Halverson deliberately stepped on the clustering mushrooms, like he was balancing rock to rock across a stream; and as he slept in the afternoon stillness, he dreamed of the mushrooms crackling under his boots. They looked poisonous, wide caps sprinkled with virulent red. Over twenty years since he had been inside this park, and now, bad dreams.

The next night they worked past the camps at the lower end of Quartz Lake, tents and the sparking remains of a fire, the end of any sort of trail. They made maybe five or six hundred yards up the north side of the lake, even with moonlight coming bright over the water, stepping along in the shallows, in and out of shadows cast by the timber, afraid their splashing would be heard by the campers down the shore where the fire still glowed. In a grassy opening between deadfalls they laid their packs against a log, and Darby unbuttoned her shirt and dropped it and stood naked to the waist. "You better get on some dry socks," Halverson said.

"I never did this before," Darby said. "I never stood like this in the moon before."

Halverson looked away. "Now is not the time for these things. You just worry about changing your socks." While he lay listening to her breathe in her sleep and watched the stars make their slow way around the moon, Halverson reflected on how long it had been since he and Darby had been after one another. The first night when he went into the tavern and she was there, tending the bar, Halverson drank late, rolling dice in a long game of Ship, Captain, and Crew; and toward closing time she looked at him and said, fine, all right she would, after she counted out the till, when he asked her if she had ever gone riding in a logging truck. Even though she invited herself into his bed after she found out he owned the truck and cabin, what they got from each other was not founded on any financial considerations; she kept her job and nobody was bought or sold. But now they were stopped, these months since spring; and maybe the way they slept without touching was causing the changes in her, thin white hands lifting her breasts in the moonlight, if she was changing and hadn't always been ready for anything, secretly. Darby was from a town named Wasco, in the great central valley of California; and her breasts were lined faintly by stretch marks. There had been other men and probably children. He wondered how much she told him, and why they could live together and not tell each other what was true.

After sunrise, picking their way along where that lone surviving girl had fought her way back toward the world, Halverson followed Darby and wished there could be some sign of that girl, a rip of cloth he could lift off a snag and tuck into his breast pocket as a sign of his intentions. But there was no hurry, and they went slowly, heading up to the swampy creekwater flat between Quartz and Cerulean Lakes, willow ground, and thick with ferns and berry brush where the bear would come to feed. Up there he would be deep below the rough high circle of hanging wall peaks, looking up to those spoon-shaped cirques carved by the ancient glaciers to the remnants of ice that would show faint white under the moon on these clear nights, and into the country where his business waited. There was no hurry and this walk was more and more a trip back into someone he had been. In the afternoon Halverson surprised himself as they stood resting on a rocky point overlooking the lake—he put his arm around Darby and held her to his side. She smelled of a deep sour odor, but it was not entirely unpleasant; it was as if all the stench from the barroom was seeping out of her. Most importantly, he was trying to figure just when he had stood in this very place before. The complex green and yellow etching of lichen on the rocks was familiar. What if you could recall even the look of the clouds from every moment of your life? There was too much of himself he was bringing along, so much he felt dizzy holding onto Darby; and he shut his mind against it.

The third night they camped a quarter mile up from Quartz Lake, toward Cerulean, north of the swampy willow ground in an open grove of stunted black cottonwood on a little knoll. The fire, their first fire, was in the ashes of another fire—where those girls might have built their fire. The beaver trappers had come into this country close to 150 years ago, when there was no one else in this high country, to this place that had no history except for the Blackfeet. But the beaver trapping must have been poor, because beaver never lived above timberline where the little creeks froze to the bottom in winter, except for the deep holes where the trout survived. There had never been enough beaver to draw the trappers. Maybe the only past here was the one he brought, him and Darby, what they remembered.

They were alone finally, up toward the head of the 15- or so mile-long valley through the ancient glacier had eroded and left for the lakes, more than 2,000 feet below the ring of peaks that had shown east of them like a crown when touched by the last sunlight. Darby was frying four small cutthroat caught from the ripple where the creek slipped into Quartz Lake when a loon called, its mournful laugh echoing over and back into the settling coolness under the mountains before moonrise, a sound Halverson had not heard since one of the far places of his childhood, but perfectly known and expected, not surprising as it came back off the shadowed walls above them. As the moon turned through the sky those shadows moved as if the mountains were going to fall out over the fire and the creekwater below.

"What were they doing here?" Darby asked.

"Who?"

"Those children." Halverson was astonished when she turned from the fire; there were tears in her eyes, lighted by the flames. "If what I'm thinking about is any of your business," she said, and she rubbed at her face and went to turn her sleeping bag open.

In the morning, Halverson set up a business of camp tending meant to last. Where they could listen to the water of the creek falling through a raft of deadwood as they perched themselves each morning after coffee, he picked a fallen barkless lodgepole to serve as toilet seat, and spooled a roll of yellow paper on a dead branch like a flag. In the afternoon he shot and butchered a yearling mule deer and ran the meat high in a tree, out of the reach of any bear, the carcass wrapped in cheesecloth to keep away the flies. In the gray light after sunset the dead animal in that white wrap of cloth turned slowly on the rope. "They ain't going to get to it," Halverson said. "But they will be coming to see."

"The bears and squirrels," Darby said. "And the park rangers. You are going to draw a crowd."

"Everybody who is interested," Halverson said. The intestines from the slaughtered yearling had been warm and slippery, and the odor of the kill had been acrid in the late-afternoon warmth. Halverson smiled for the first time, smelling his hands, where the faint odor of deer remained.

How long had he refused returning into these mountains? Why had that girl come here from that rich place on the outskirts of Columbus, Ohio? Why come hunting a place where there is no one else? The girl had used the excuse of school for getting away from whatever crowded life she had been born to, then quit her wild-life biology studies down in Missoula and gone off to Columbia Falls with that boy who delivered cocaine and climbed in the summer, and now she was dead in these mountains.

"What do you guess she was up to?" Halverson said.

"You wait and you wait," Darby said, "and everything takes all the time it can. Then it all comes in a hurry." She shook salt over the venison steaks in the frying pan. "You . . ." she said and waited. "Why don't you ever fuck me?"

"Why are you talking like shit?" Halverson said. "You tell me what fucking has to do with this?"

"Nothing. I'm just wondering. She never talked any-thing serious to me, like I never knew anything, or come from anywhere, and all the time I could have told her."

"You could have told her what?"

"About how we go looking for some one thing to be, and there's nothing to find."

The biggest trouble, he understood, was that he was not afraid. Halverson tried to center himself into that frail girl, the girl who died, and then he shook his head. He wished he had brought a pint of whiskey so that this single night, when everything was ready, he could rest here with his common sense turning circles and be inside that girl and feeling the warmth from this fire and the cool night on her back, drifting in someone else—a rich girl estranged from the rich part of Ohio—and no rifle.

Maybe that would have worked—no rifle. At least he might have been a little bit afraid and not sitting here with thoughts of his dead father, and his mother living her life out in San Diego. His mother in a wicker chair on the front lawn and sunset over the warships in San Diego harbor; Halverson saw her, and some dim memory of his father kneeling in the snow to fasten the straps on her snowshoes, a logging road and larch in the background.

"Why don't you ever?" Darby said.

"What?"

"You know."

"Because you talk like you do."

Picking along the edge where the lodgepole timber leveled into the swamp, scouting the new territory, Halverson was walking alone when the old she-bear reared herself out of thick brush only a hundred or so yards before him. Listening but no doubt unable to make him out with her weak eyes, she was maybe ready to come at him and find out what he was, but more likely to drop and lope away. Halverson heard her snuffling; and as he had planned, but before he was able to understand this was not what he wanted, not this easiness, he centered the crosshairs just beneath her dark uplifted nose and fired. As he slipped his finger across the trigger, he was astonished by the noise, which hadn't mattered when he'd killed the doe, the hard jolt of the rifle stock against his shoulder and the crack that went echoing, the massive head jerking away, gone from the scope. Halverson thought he had missed, levered in another shell, thinking *nowhere*, then lifted his eye from the scope to see the bear floundering backward and sideways into the leafy brush, and falling as he had imagined. With such thoughtless luck he was done with it now and had killed his grizzly, too quickly for recall, except for the diminishing echo of the rifle shot; and he was already sorry, knowing this one was wasted. There had to be another, stalked and properly confronted and then killed. There had to be time for thinking, and time for the bear, for hoping the animal might dimly sense the thing happening.

Halverson waited, listening, expecting Darby, who did not come, hearing nothing but the buzz of insects. Soon the birds began moving and calling in the trees once more, and then he went to the bear. The odor was rancid, and Halverson was surprised by the smallness of the dead animal, the raggedness of her coat, because already he could see it was a she-bear, an old one who looked to be shedding in midsummer, the gray-tipped pelt ragged and almost slick to the hide around the rear haunches. An old one. The wrong one. The .458 magnum slug had entered her mouth and blown away the back of her skull. Halverson cupped his fingers into the wound and there was nothing to be felt but pulpy flesh and sharp bone fragments and warm blood, like thick soup.

He tasted the salty blood.

Kneeling beside the carcass, Halverson tried again to think of the dead girl in these mountains. The stench of the animal beside him was like a part of the air. Off in the willows a frog was croaking; and then he heard the first sounds of the helicopter, rotor blades cutting at the stillness as the aircraft came up along the length of Quartz Lake, the thunking louder until the helicopter hung between the walls of the stippled rock face above him.

Downstream that roll of yellow toilet paper was spooled onto the dead branch like a flag. The helicopter turned and lifted, moved half a mile away. Halverson brought the rifle to his shoulder and through the eye of the scope watched the two men up there searching for him with binoculars. Don't find me, Halverson thought. This is none of your business, and it is not finished. We are not in this together.

It had to have been the echoing of the shot that drew the men in the helicopter. The afternoon of the day before he'd killed the yearling mule deer; and now, another shot, echoing down the length of the lake, they were after him. Only when the helicopter lifted and turned in three wide fluttering circles and then bore off down the lake, going away, did Halverson pay attention to what came next. He would have to build a silencer.

Darby would not leave. "You got me here," she said, "so you are going to have trouble getting me out, even if they come looking." She was talking about the park-service rangers. "There won't be the rifle, so there is nothing against the law about me being here." The carcass of the gutted doe was hanging a quarter mile away, wrapped in cheesecloth. Halverson thought of that, but didn't say anything. Let her learn, if this is what she wants. Halverson went out of the park the next morning, carrying only the rifle, and drove back to his cabin in the canyon above Columbia Falls. Even without the pack it was a hard daylong march. Darby would be all right, or else she wouldn't. She had insisted on coming along, and she was into it.

The silencer turned out to be a reasonably simple piece of business. Halverson slipped an eight-inch section of the heavy plastic hot-water tubing over thick rubber washers on the end of the rifle barrel; and when it was securely in place, he cut pipe threads on the outside of the tubing. This was a mount for the silencer. The thing itself consisted of two cylinders, a small perforated core of metal tubing inside a larger section of steel pipe, the space between them packed with sound-absorbing steel wool. Halverson brazed it together in the pole-walled shed back of his cabin, where he kept the Kenworth in winter, then screwed the silencer onto the threaded plastic pipe fixed to the end of the rifle barrel. It was like a small metal can hanging out there. He fired the rifle into the hillside back of the cabin, and the contraption worked. There was the crack of the magnum slug passing the sound barrier, he lost none of his muzzle velocity, but the explosive roar was absorbed in the steel wool. He was ready again. This time he would hunt quietly, secretly, and choose and get this properly done with. He called and had the telephone shut off, and the power, and the newspaper. Through it all he felt as if he were acting on precise instructions for going away that he did not need to understand. That night he thought of Darby up there alone in her sleeping bag, the frogs croaking in the darkness. He wondered if she was frightened, or if she was walking around naked amid the trees. If she touched herself in the night, who would she be thinking about? Before driving back to the park in the morning, he went into Columbia Falls and bought a newspaper to read with breakfast; and again acting on what seemed to be directives for survival somewhere else, a guidebook to species of edible mushrooms.

Darby had moved the camp. She found another fire ring a couple of miles upstream from their first camp, and said the ashes were fresh and no doubt it was the place where the girls had camped. "It was the right place, being here where they were," she said. Halverson had found her late in the afternoon, and now it was dark.

"Which one will you be?" Darby said. "One night you can be one, and I'll be the other, and then we can switch around. We can see which one gets eaten worst." She smiled as though this lewdness was very funny, and turned back to her work, frying three trout. "Maybe this is the place. When I was here alone, I tried to think what that girl was thinking, and it felt like the place."

"What did she think?"

But Darby didn't answer, and Halverson took the whiskey from his day-pack. Along with the book on mushrooms, he had brought a quart of Jack Daniel's. The firelight shone through the liquid like a dim lantern. "There was a man here, really a boy, the second night you were gone," Darby said. "One of those park-service boys, just last year out of college in Vermont. He was looking for you. At least he was looking for someone with a rifle. He was frightened. That's what he said. Probably some lunatic son of a bitch, is what he said. I didn't say anything. I don't think he wanted to find anybody, least of all a man." She salted the frying fish. "He talked about how this park is open ground for crazies. What he said is lunatics. He said there was no control, and lunatics clustered in places where there was no control."

"Maybe he got it right. We might stay here forever. All the goddamned helicopters do no good. We might stay right here," Halverson said. "You know what I did? You guess . . . I got back and there was a week's newspapers all over the porch." He was going to lie, there had been the newspapers, but the rest of this was going to be a lie. "I didn't call them and have the newspaper shut off, or the power company shut off the lights, or the telephone. Those things are going on back there, without us, to remind them. I could have shut it off, but I didn't." Halverson waited for her to look away from the fire and back toward him.

"Who are they reminding?" Darby said. "About what?"

When Halverson didn't answer, she went on. "What I did is, I slept with that boy. In his sleeping bag and mine zipped together. He was frightened and I felt like his mother, holding onto him all night." Darby finally turned and looked at Halverson. "It was the right thing to do," she said.

"Did you fuck him?"

She nodded. She did not seem disturbed. "It was the right thing to do. I wanted to be with somebody, and it made him feel better."

Halverson was not frightened, and he was not angry. Maybe she did do the right thing, for her. It was not anything he could get himself to think about. "I guess we could have a drink together," Halverson said. Maybe each thing they were doing was the right thing to do. He poured them each a shot in the steel Sierra Club cups and didn't say anything about how he was going to sit drunk in the night and see if he could see what it could maybe feel like to be that girl as the bear began nudging at the tent walls. He would get drunk and think he was alone and begin whimpering; and when he woke up and the hangover was gone, he would begin hunting.

Late in the night, sipping at his whiskey and sharpening his skinning knife by firelight, Halverson surprised himself. Darby was curled in her sleeping bag, maybe sleeping and maybe not, when Halverson for the first time in all this surprised himself absolutely by drawing the knife along the tender flesh inside his left forearm, careful to avoid the veins as they stood out, just softly tracing and watching the painless slide of the blade and the immediate welling streak of blood, holding himself so he did not force the blade deeper, pulling away just as he reached the wrist. After a moment of watching the blood gather and begin to drip, he held the knife low over the coals until the cutting edge began to glow red, and then breathing through his teeth, he seared the wound. The next morning, when Darby asked, he told her it had only been a test.

"Just practicing, I thought about cutting off a finger," he said, which was a lie, "but then I thought, there is nothing to grieve over, so I didn't cut off no finger."

"That's fine," Darby said.

"The first blood," Halverson said, "was always mine."

"Never in the world," Darby said. "That story I told, about fucking with that boy, was a lie. I've had plenty of that. It didn't happen."

What Halverson did not tell her was that the whiskey worked: he finally dreamed of the girl who died. At least it was a dream he had never witnessed before, and it must have come from someone nearby. It must have been waiting. Below in some street there was the snow melting as it fell on wet black asphalt that flared under the headlights of a red Olds convertible that was backing out of a long driveway. In the street, the convertible did not move. The motor stopped and the headlights dimmed, and Halverson, in his sleep, thought: which window is this I am watching from?

Then he was awake and the fire was burned down to embers; and he listened to the snapping of pitch and Darby's breathing, and he heard the rasping of brush against brush and stillness; and knew it was the girl's dream he was in because for the first time he was afraid. The rifle was there, he could touch it by reaching out, but he was trembling.

Another sound, and he lay there, not calling out to Darby because this was not her business, feeling his forearms tremble as a pine limb flared, and waiting for the rooting hog-like sound that never came. There was a whisper of air high in the yellow pine. The moon was

gone. Off east the high wall of the cirque hung in delicate outline against the fainter blue of what had to be
the sky turning toward morning. Nothing had happened,
and as the dream began to fade there was nothing to do
but rebuild the fire.

After breakfast, as she watched him scrubbing their
plates with sand in the cold water at the edge of the
stream, Darby got started talking about what was fair.
She wanted seriously to try the rifle, not just firing off at
nothing on a hillside, but killing. "You slice at your arm
like that, you might cut your throat. Where would I be,
when there was trouble?"

"What would you kill?"

Darby didn't answer, but turned her back to Halverson, unbuttoned her wrinkled blue work shirt, dropped
it off her shoulders, and sat facing the morning sun on
a grassy ledge above the creek, slumping, as from the
weight of her breasts. "No wonder you draw crowds,"
Halverson said, "sitting around bare-assed like that."

"Maybe I already did. Maybe I had a boatload of cow-
boys, and there is more coming in tonight, and maybe I
am just warning you." The stretch marks on her breasts
and over her hips were a silvery network in the light. So I
was never pretty, she said, after their first night together,
talking about the marks, tracing them with a fingertip
after she turned on a light, showing them to him like
some wound, but never explaining. I never been pretty
because of these, she said, and he never asked where they
came from.

"You are going to sunburn your tits," Halverson said,
and he went off to the half-rotten cored-out deadfall
where he kept the rifle hidden. Quietly he slipped a
cartridge into the firing chamber and raised the rifle and

fired without aiming, as she had that morning behind the cabin, only he was firing toward the grayish snowpack in the ravines on Redhorn Peak.

"I heard you," she said when he came back to where she sat in the sun. Halverson was carrying the rifle and her shirt was on and unbuttoned. "You missed," she said, and she looked around and bit at the tip of her index finger as she watched him eject the empty casing. Halverson put in another shell.

"Not now," she said. "I changed my mind."

There were no clouds anywhere in the long sky reaching off south and west from the peaks; and far off in the trough to the west, Quartz Lake shone under the late-afternoon sun. Early that morning, standing over the darkness of Cerulean Lake, Halverson had looked down from the logjam at the creek outlet to trees floating upright far below the surface, his face mirrored among them, then spent the morning climbing along the southern rise of the drainage. He was resting in the noontime warmth on a rotting log, listening to the silence that whispered of insects, when he heard the dry cracking of a limb breaking. A fragile dead branch stepped on and snapped, that sound, from back the way he had come before breaking out onto this open burn-slope.

But this was Darby, not a bear. She had followed him all this way. Halverson watched as she came from the timber into the sunlight maybe 150 yards down-slope, stopped and looked around and didn't see him. Halverson watched as she undid the buttons on her blue work shirt again, took it off and knotted the sleeves around her waist. This time she was wearing the orange top to her swimming suit over her breasts. Watching her through the scope on the rifle, the magnification bringing her up to only fifteen or so yards, Halverson was surprised how tanned she was from this last couple of weeks lying naked in the afternoons while he was off hunting. There it was, this other person she had become. What was she following, all this way into his idea of what he had to do?

It was Darby, after he whistled softly to her and waved, who first saw the bear. She sat beside him on the rotting log, not saying anything, as if there was no reason to explain why she spent this long day trailing him, and then she said, "Do you see him?"

"Who?"

"Down over there."

There it was, down the length of her pointing arm, the bear thrashing lazily in the berry brush, head down and only the dark hump flashing at them occasionally. Halverson watched through the scope, and saw the animal roll a great rotting log for the grubs on the underside, the casual movement of enormous strength like that of a man moving driftwood on a beach. This sunny quiet day. Halverson wondered what he should do now, which move to make. Rest the rifle solidly on the log, shout, and when the animal stands, breathe one last deep steady time, and fire. That is how close you must be. It was all too easy.

"What you can do is go down there with your knife," Darby said. "You can slide up closer and closer, and I will do the shooting."

"Yeah, sure," Halverson said.

"Otherwise there's no point. We can shoot him right now and go home, if that's all you want, to kill a bear." She wet her index finger and marked a cross in the air. "That does it. One bear." He understood she wanted something more than he did. What did she want?

Halverson understood what he was going to do. Darby

was right, this was not any kind of getting even, and making things even was not what he was about. *He didn't want me.* Those were the words of the girl who survived. As if the bear possessed some gift, and had withheld it from her.

"See if you can do it," Halverson said, and he slid a cartridge into the firing chamber and handed the rifle to Darby. She took it like she had been waiting. Halverson gave her three cartridges. "See if you can do it," he said again.

Only when he was fifty or so yards downhill, with his skinning knife in his right hand, did Halverson wonder at all about what he was doing. He could feel the eye of the scope on his back, and as he moved carefully through the brush, Halverson thought, *now who is the hunter?*

Not even yet was he afraid. He had been afraid in the night, after dreaming, when he lay in his sleeping bag and trembled and nothing happened but the eventual sunrise. But that was gone, and nothing was left of the terrible anger he felt the first night in his cabin, if it was anger, when he heard the girl was dead. Halverson felt small and weak, but not afraid. Brilliant deep pinkish lavender stalks of fireweed grew waist high from long-rotted roots of an overturned alpine fir. Puffball mushrooms, overripe by now, clustered under them. Halverson bent and punctured the gray-white skin of a mushroom with a forefinger. It had looked like a little balloon on the ground. The skin broke; the spores rose like gunpowder smoke. The odor of the spores was that of clean earth, slightly acid, as was the taste when he licked his forefinger. Halverson felt himself touching one thing at a time with great slowness. The rasp of a wasp in the air before him was abrasive against his eyelids as he hesitated. One thing and then another. He moved carefully over the spongy lichen-covered and mossy ground between clumps of deep saw-edged grass, crouching and pushing through slowly, reaching for one of the red-purple berries that hung in clusters around him, tasting it, pulling a handful that were sticky in his palm as he crouched there eating them one at a time. The after-taste was like a sour ache in his mouth. So, he thought, this is the way you are feeding.

Halverson stood quiet amid the buzzing of insects, lis-tening. He heard the bear stirring just ahead in the brush. The smell of it was like an odor of clean rot in the sunlight, tangible as something to taste, the air filled with bright floating specks like infinitesimal crystalline butterflies that would settle and flutter on the tongue after drifting on currents of light. He could hear the bear's chuffing—a grunting sound that was more like slow, heavy breath-ing rather than anything eating. Only when he moved closer, crouching again and stepping forward slowly, did Halverson at last see the animal. Low to the ground, look-ing upward through leafy green brush, he saw the dark belly and realized he was being watched. The grunting had stopped and Halverson looked up and saw the bear reared and gazing down on him, black lips curled over the fangs as though the animal were smiling, and nothing but curious.

The bear shook its head against the flies crawling on its lips in the thick juice of the berries. Halverson stepped back and stood upright, seeing that shake of the animal's head as an acknowledgment, almost a greeting. Halverson was not sure what to do except wait; he was this close, he should always have been this close. The bear lifted its muzzle, weaving its head from side to side, looking upward as if there might be some tiny thing to be seen far off in the sky, then lowered its head and dropped slowly forward, the decision made, and after a great slow bunching of itself, moved at him, hidden a moment in the brush, and then at him, before him. The leaves shook as if there had been a wind to accompany the rush. The animal stopped and reared again. Halverson lifted the knife.

With forelegs raised, the bear looked down at him. The dark eyes were soft, and the terrible odor was a stench. With the knife still upraised, Halverson waited: *this close.*

What do you do with the knife? Do you step closer, toward the embrace, and where do you plunge the blade? There was no knowing; Halverson began to move forward, stroking the blade of the knife through the air with small tentative motions while he waited to know what he should do as the bear lifted its forelegs higher, and then Halverson was no longer wondering as in the slowness of what happened he tasted the sweet fecal breath of the animal, Halverson touching his tongue to his teeth. One thing and then another. The clean long pelt over the breast of the animal was ruffled by what had to have been a breeze in the afternoon stillness. Softly it ruffled, like a woman's hair as Halverson tried to imagine it later, except that it was really like nothing but that yellowish silver flutter before him, not like a woman's hair at all. And then there was a shot, the crack as the lead slug from the rifle broke over his head, the flat splattering sound; and Halverson saw what he had been unable to imagine, the head jerking back, the terrible involuntary slackness as the jaws gaped open, the spasm in the eyes, the flowering of blood, and the bear going down in the brush, dead with a great final rush of breath.

Halverson lowered his knife. There was nothing to defend against; there hadn't been, not unless he courted it, and the anger he felt, the trembling in his forearms,

was not so much at anything as it was at loss; and he did
not know what was lost. He stood over the bear, now
a mere dead animal, however large, and looked at his
knife. There is the least you can manage, he thought,
and dropped to his knees, enveloped in the hot stench,
and began hacking, dismembering, cutting off the head.
It was a long job, and he broke the knife blade prying
between the vertebrae, but finally the head rolled free, a
couple of turns down the slope, coming to rest beneath
the clusters of red-purple berries.

When Halverson stood, his back ached and his arms
and chest were sloppy from his wallowing at his job, in
the blood. All the time feeling the scope on his back,
Halverson rested and smoked a cigarette, and then with
his arms wrapped awkwardly around it, smelling it,
Halverson began transporting the head back up the slope
to Darby. He wondered fleetingly if she would let him
reach her. At last she lowered the rifle.

"I waited long enough, didn't I?" she asked. He stood
before her, legs braced against the fleshy weight of the
head. She stood on the grayish rotting log where she had
rested the rifle, which she had let fall into the matted
grass. Halverson set the head at her feet, so it grinned up
at them—great carnivorous teeth closed and the black
lips slack. He dropped the broken knife, watching it fall
through the tangled grass to the mossy ground. "That
will do," he said. The head of the bear could rest there
on that log, the insects could have it until it was a skull,
looking west.

Halverson brushed away a fly that was crawling on
the fingers of his left hand. Seven cartridges were heavy
in the loops of his belt. One by one he took them out
and fired them away toward the peaks; the crack, the
rush of the slug, then nothing. All this was one act of

trust after another. The far white sky to the west was reflected from the lake below in its trough. They were inside a place where each thing irrevocably followed another, and the only hesitations were those that could be reckoned with.

Back at their camp Halverson fired the rest of the cartridges, then gave Darby the rifle and asked her to take it out and hide it in some place where it couldn't be found.

"You know that old one, that cripple the rangers killed," she said. "Well, they killed the right one. The belly was full of hair."

Halverson told her that didn't make any difference. He built a fire and sat with his back to it, watching the line of shadow rise on the peaks as the sun descended. Then he heard her coming back. "Darby," he said.

"I'm here," she said.

WILLIAM KITTREDGE grew up on and then managed his family's cattle ranch in eastern Oregon. He studied in the Writers' Workshop at the University of Iowa, and became the Regents Professor of English and Creative Writing at the University of Montana until retiring in 1997. He has received numerous prestigious awards including a Stegner Fellowship at Stanford, two Writing Fellowships from the NEA, and two Pacific Northwest Bookseller's Awards for Excellence. He was co-producer of the movie *A River Runs Through It*. Kittredge has published in more than 50 magazines and newspapers, among them the *Atlantic, Harper's, Esquire, Time, Newsweek, TriQuarterly,* the *Paris Review,* the *Washington Post,* the *New York Times,* and the *Los Angeles Times.* His books include *Who Owns The West?; A Hole in the Sky; The Nature of Generosity; Taking Care: Thoughts on Storytelling and Belief; The Van Gogh Field;* and *We Are Not in This Together.* With Annick Smith, he edited *The Last Best Place: A Montana Anthology.*

The text of this book has been set in Berling,
a typeface designed by the Swedish typographer
and calligrapher Karl-Erik Forsberg.

Book design by Wendy Holdman.
Typesetting by Stanton Publication Services, Inc.
Manufactured by Friesens on acid-free paper.

Graywolf Press is a not-for-profit, independent press. The books we publish include poetry, literary fiction, essays, and cultural criticism. We are less interested in best-sellers than in talented writers who display a freshness of voice coupled with a distinct vision. We believe these are the very qualities essential to shape a vital and diverse culture.

Thankfully, many of our readers feel the same way. They have shown this through their desire to buy books by Graywolf writers; they have told us this themselves through their e-mail notes and at author events; and they have reinforced their commitment by contributing financial support, in small amounts and in large amounts, and joining the "Friends of Graywolf."

If you enjoyed this book and wish to learn more about Graywolf Press, we invite you to ask your bookseller or librarian about further Graywolf titles; or to contact us for a free catalog; or to visit our award-winning web site that features information about our forthcoming books.

We would also like to invite you to consider joining the hundreds of individuals who are already "Friends of Graywolf" by contributing to our membership program. Individual donations of any size are significant to us: they tell us that you believe that the kind of publishing we do matters. Our web site gives you many more details about the benefits you will enjoy as a "Friend of Graywolf"; but if you do not have online access, we urge you to contact us for a copy of our membership brochure.

www. graywolfpress.org

Graywolf Press
2402 University Avenue, Suite 203
Saint Paul, MN 55114
Phone: (651) 641-0077
Fax: (651) 641-0036
E-mail: wolves@graywolfpress.org